CLAIMED

BY THE

WEREWOLF BOSS

ASH RAVEN

100% HUMAN MADE
100% HUMAN MADE
I SUPPORT HUMAN
CREATORS AND MAKERS
NO AI WAS USED IN THE
CREATION OF THIS BOOK

CONTENTS

STORY INTRODUCTION

At a destination wedding for her best friend, Cheyenne Walker is on a mission to relax, support the bride, and hopefully cure her creative burnout. But from the moment she sees him, she's caught in the strange thralls of Valentino Benetti and the whirlwind, book boyfriend inspiring romance he takes her on. Little does she know, he's hiding more than just his connection to the mafia.

With a rat in his organisation and the chaos of a wedding at his family villa, the last thing Valentino expected to find was a fated mate. He's determined to claim Cheyenne and show her what life with him will be like all before his nephew's big day.

But what happens if the rat gets to her first?

CONTENT

Content: Instant obsession, Italian holiday romance, plus size main characters, slight author meta

Triggers: Dark themes, blood and gore, torture, murder, cannibalism, kidnapping, light stalking, organised crime

Sex Related: Breeding kink (***no pregnancy***), light degredation, light somnophilia, oral (FMC and MMC receiving), power exchange dynamics, sex toys, knotting, dubious mate bonding, transformed sex

Valentino

I shouldn't linger when my nephew and a few of the boys are waiting for me to kill a rat. But what can I say? When you've been the head of the Benetti Crime Family for twenty-five years, you know not to relax, even at your nonna's villa in the old country. There is something in the wind tonight that makes the fur running down my back stand on end. My claws dig into the damp soil as I sniff the air again.

The peonies are starting to bloom around the tall stone walls, mixing with the climbing roses, but beneath that there is something unfamiliar. A deep musk that draws me away from the woods where my pack is waiting for me, and instead towards the front gate. My tail twitches as it gets closer, more defined. It's feminine, a little sweaty, and oh so fucking delicious. Drool forms in the back of my long jaws, dripping down my extended canines.

The wolf part of me wants to track this scent down and claim them right here, right now. Hunt them, chase them, tackle them into the dirt and fuck my knot into their hole until they are crying for me. I want to taste them, their blood dripping from my jowls while I mate them. How pretty will they scream for me when I ruin them? Arousal, feral and hot, pumps through me uncontrollably until my cock pulses and drips precum onto the ground beneath me.

I wrap a clawed hand around my knot and squeeze the aching flesh. I can't leave my family waiting for too long, but I can't ignore this.

Whoever this smell belongs to, belongs to me now. Nothing will stop me from having whoever this person is, not a spouse, not a partner, not a fucking vow of celibacy will prevent me from claiming them. I've never smelt anyone so divine, who's had me dropping on all fours to race to them. My body breaks through branches, my large paws crushing leaves and twigs without care.

The closer I get, the more distinct their scent is. Sweat, weed, powdery deodorant, and bubble gum fill my snout. My heart races as I push harder, desperate to get to this person. The wolf in me wants to howl, announce to the pack and all of Italy that I've found a mate at long last.

I skid to a stop as we meet half a mile from the gate entrance.

A gorgeous and dishevelled creature grunts as they tug a large suitcase up the hill. Their sandals slap against their feet with each step, announcing them to the world. They huff and puff but keep moving. I stalk them through the tree line. My cock aches being so close to them, but I can't just fucking shift and step into the road naked. I also can't reveal this part of myself to a stranger. The secrets of the Benetti pack are for made men and mates.

And if I have my way, this plump little morsel will be mated to me before it's even time to come home.

I kick a rock into the street. They look over their shoulders quickly, eyes scanning the tree line. They don't stop moving, but their breath stutters for a moment. Their heart rate picks up that little bit more, and I bite back a whimper. Whoever this is, heading right into my fucking den, has me aching in a way I never have before.

They pull out their phone and shine a light into the trees. They must see my eyes, the glow of them, how they reflect when they move the torch over me. My lips pull back in a snarl when they turn it off again, plunging them back into the dark. They should leave it on, it's already dangerous to be walking up the road in the dark like this.

What if someone decides they are an easy target? A beautiful being like them with all those round, fat curves on display? I would happily snatch them off the road just to drown in those tits and feel those plush thighs squeeze my hips while I fuck into their hole.

Jesus, I need to get my mate into the villa and get my shit together.

They are a person who deserves my fucking respect, then my nasty fantasies. Being shifted like this skews my thoughts too much, makes me more of the monster I am. Like this, I want to breed them, fuck as much of my cum into them until they are ripe with my pups. Shit, they might not even be able to have kids or want them, but I want to fucking try anyway.

I hope they have a breeding kink.

My mate walks up to the security guard outside of the villa, and I'm already changing. They better not fucking talk to Dino too long. I'll have to fucking kill him. He's been a good man, a good soldier who wants to be more than a made man one day. My mate shows him their phone, and he smiles that fucking schoolboy smile of his and lets them through the gate.

The moment it closes, I step out of the trees and prowl up to him. The wild side of me wants to rip his fucking head off with my bare hands for looking at my mate. The rational side of me knows that's stupid and a waste of a good soldier.

"Hey boss, you alright?" he asks, unfazed by my nudity. You get used to it or you get buried around here.

"Who was that?" I demand.

"Ms Walker? She's on Junelle's list for the wedding. She's the last guest to arrive for the weekend."

He says it so casually. She's on Junelle's list. My mate is so close with my nephew's fiance she was invited all the way out to our family's villa for the wedding. Well, second wedding, the first one was in Jamaica where Junelle's family is from. Andrea had asked me two years ago if I would be open to having two ceremonies, as if I would ever say no to Junelle. That woman is a gift from God. She and Andrea are perfect for each other even beyond the mate bond that werewolves form.

They share something so deep and beautiful that even the heavens weep for them.

Something I used to wish for when I was a young man like Andrea, something I never thought I would have.

Until tonight.

"What's her file like?" I ask Dino, refocusing on my mate in the here and now, and not the what-ifs of the future.

"Basic, she and Junelle went to college together."

He hands his tablet over to me, and I thumb through the documents we have on her. Cheyenne Walker, red hair, brown eyes, five-five, 230 pounds, no restrictions on her driving licence. She's freshly turned thirty and a middle school teacher from Tolson with a district-level award for teaching. No kids, no close family, no partners. She doesn't even have a single traffic violation under her name.

My mate is downright boring according to this file. She goes to work, she goes home, and sometimes she goes to the art museum.

Fuck is that going to make this difficult. Boring people don't take risks or date questionable men. They certainly don't look kindly on mobsters transforming into seven-foot-tall werewolves who like to maim and kill and fuck while they are still covered in blood.

"Should I keep an eye on her, Mr Benetti?" Dino's question pops me out of a spiralling kidnapping plan that involves tying my girl up and breaking her into a million pieces until she only knows what way is up because I tell her so.

"No," I bark too quickly. "No, she's Junelle's friend, treat her with respect. This is a wedding, ain't it?"

Dino is definitely not convinced by my reaction, but he's been around long enough to know to keep his mouth shut. I say goodbye and transform back into my wolf. I've got shit to do. Being the boss doesn't allow for distractions like this. My mate is safe, she's surrounded by my family, people I trust with my life. I will hunt her down in the morning.

For now, I've got a rat to squeeze.

The run should have done me some good. Besides the fact that I could always use some more exercise, finding Cheyenne has clouded all my thoughts. As I approach the small hunting cabin that hasn't been used for that purpose in decades, I recentre myself on the task at hand. I can't let on to Andrea that I've found my mate at his wedding. This is a big weekend for him. I don't want to overshadow it.

Outside the cabin, Ugo stands guard outside of our rat cage with a suit bag draped over his shoulders.

I'm not sure how the little human shit stain who runs one of our swimming piers was able to get enough information to have one of our capos locked up stateside, but I'm going to find out. As an associate, he's not in the know. He's not a made man, and he most certainly ain't a fucking wolf. Which means we are going to start our little interrogation in human form.

"Hey, boss," Ugo grins, canines sharper and deadlier. He is my go-to guy for scaring the shit out of people who don't want to pay up or shut up. He's a killer through and through, but a loyal enforcer I'd trust with my life.

"How was the drive up?" I make chitchat before I shift down. I've got to refocus my wolf on the task at hand before I can turn human again.

There aren't two fucking wolves inside me. That is some fucking Grade A bullshit. Werewolves aren't born, they are made, just like all the people in our little syndicate. The transformation changes you physically, emotionally, mentally. It brings out all your traits as a person, but it also adds more beastly ones. And those new ones sometimes try to run the show.

Like now.

"Fine, ya know how it goes." Ugo shrugs. "They scream, they fight, they beg. Andrea and Junelle were on the phone the whole drive up, discussing flower arrangements while he fucking cried in the background. I thought she was gonna come out here and rip his fucking throat out herself."

This is yet another shining example of why Junelle is perfect for Andrea. My nephew, second in line for head of the Benetti family, is a soft guy. He likes things to be neat, solved with a bit of conversation and maybe a contract being signed. His parents wanted him raised book smart, God rest their souls, but he's not a killer. Junelle will slit a man's throat over the brunch table if he gets in her way.

How did Cheyenne and Junelle ever become friends? College roommates doesn't automatically mean friends for life. My new niece doesn't trust easily, but that could just be my assumption based on the circumstances of our introduction.

It's not something I enjoy doing, but I force the change. Ugo throws the bag at me, and I put on my black suit. It's a bit warm for it, but appearance matters in cases like this. I slap Ugo on the shoulder and head inside.

The air is stale with hydrogen peroxide. Humans can't smell it, but it lingers after a clean-up. Andrea and Marcello, our capo based here in Italy who is also my second cousin on my father's side, play cards at a small garden table. The shit stain hangs from a chain in the ceiling. His sandals scrape against the tiled floor as he swings slowly, whimpering and muttering a prayer through his split lip.

"You get lost, Tino?" Andrea smirks as reveals his hand, a full house.

Marcello falls back into his chair with a groan, before tossing his watch at my nephew. Okay, maybe he's soft, but he's a bit of a card shark. Not like any of us have played fair before in our life, why start with a game of cards?

"Just some business at the villa," I explain, giving him a look. He rolls his eyes. We both know I won't say anything in front of the rat until his still-beating heart is stomped flat under my boot.

"Junelle won't like that," he hums. "I've already had to give her bad news tonight."

"What's the problem?"

"The florist isn't trying hard enough, so I need to have a little chat with them," he says quickly. "Nothing for you to worry about."

A smirk forms on my lips. Yeah, I've seen how a chat from Andrea can change a man's mind. Whatever they're fucking up, the florist will soon have a different tune to sing.

"Giuseppe here would like to explain himself, boss." Marcello brings us back to business. "He is very, very sorry."

The rat nods. I get a closer look at him under the light, see the tear tracks lining his cheeks, the swelling around his jaw. The boys have roughed him up a bit, but it's nothing serious yet, nothing permanent.

"How long have you worked for us?"

"Ten years, Mr Benetti," he whispers, struggling to form the words in English.

"Were we not treating you well?" I switch to Italian.

"Yes, I mean no, no, you treat me very well, sir." He flinches when I take off my jacket.

I'd rather not ruin my suit tonight. The family is used to blood, to seeing us covered in it for whatever reason, but I can't risk running into Cheyenne covered in blood.

"Then what changed, friend? Who sunk their claws into you and offered something better?"

The chains overhead rattle as he begins to shake. Like prey caught in a trap, the danger he's in really starts to sink in. This isn't a beating and you go home, this isn't even spilling his guts for talking to the pigs. This is going to send a violent and painful message to everyone in our village.

Nobody fucks with the Benettis.

"He-he said he could get me moved up the family," he explains. "More than a made man."

My eyes flick to the others. It's not usually a risk we face. The pack is bound to secrecy, bound to each other. Our continued existence as wolves relies on keeping our fucking yaps shut. There's always someone who thinks they can double-cross us, another family who thinks they can drop one of their sons or daughters into our ranks to spy on us.

But one of our own breaking rank and pack like this? It's so fucking unfathomable, I can barely keep myself from changing. The rage, the fear for my loved ones, surges through my veins faster than my heart can beat.

"Who told you?" I demand.

"I can't," he whispers.

I grab hold of his throat before he takes his next breath. His dark eyes widen, his lips tremble as he tries to draw in air. My hand shifts, claws extending into his soft jugular. That little pinprick of awareness flashes across his face. Like he sees the wolf I truly am.

"Who told you?" My canines extend again and my mouth widens.

"The alpha," he gasps.

Andrea chokes while Marcello snorts with laughter. That is a debunked load of crap from a quack scientist studying wolves in captivity. Not how wolf packs work in the wild, and it certainly isn't how werewolves work.

We are a fucking family. I may sit at the head of the table, but we are a unit that thrives on supporting each other.

"Who is that?" I taunt our rat, pushing him so he swings while I circle him. He drags ragged breath after ragged breath as I remove more of my clothes. He watches, piss dripping down his legs. Jesus, he needs to drink more water.

The leather of my belt slaps together hard. "Who's the alpha?"

"I only ever saw the monster," he sobs, squeezing his eyes shut.

"Did he look like this?"

I transform, muscles stretching, bones breaking and mending, and hair bursting through my skin.

My stupid tail even pops out like a jack-in-the-box, wagging and ready for blood.

Giuseppe screams and cries when he looks at me under the light. I snarl at him. His heart beats too hard, like it's about to give out. Maybe he's having a panic attack.

"Who is the alpha?" I ask one last time, fist wrapping around the chain and pulling him up to my eye level. I place my other hand over his heart.

"I can't—"

My claws break through his chest cavity before he can finish that same pathetic line.

The rat chokes as blood dribbles out of his mouth and around my fist. The colour drains from him and coats my grey fur. Sick and hungry satisfaction hums in my veins as I push a little harder into his body, reaching for his heart. How long will he survive this? Can I make him see his still-beating heart?

I'm not a surgeon on a good day. My claws sink into the organ, and I yank. Blood vessels and arteries stretch like elastic until they snap, spraying blood across me and the room. He probably died the moment I touched his heart, but I don't care. He wasn't planning to tell me who this alpha fucker is.

His blood is hot on my tongue when I devour his heart, chewing and crushing the muscle between my sharp fangs. He doesn't quell the fury I feel. It sinks in my gut while his useless corpse hangs there.

"Shit, Tino," Andrea chuckles. "Turning more animal than man these days."

I resist the urge to shake the blood off my fur, licking my snout.

Marcello calls Ugo in, and they work to unchain the rat and drag him outside. They'll dump him somewhere for people to see, to send a message to our other associates that this is what happens to those who think they can back out of our agreement, who think they can be better than a Benetti. I'll call our friends down at the morgue tomorrow morning. The wild boars in the area have gone a bit wild, what can I say?

"What was the hold-up earlier?" Andrea asks once the room is clear.

"The last guest arrived while I was doing a walk-around, Cheyenne Walker?"

I try to hold in my emotions when I say her name. The desire and hunger I have for her has already sunk its claws deeper into me than I just had in Giuseppe. After the wedding, I tell myself over and over again.

"Oh, nice." My nephew smiles. "Haven't seen her in a while, explains why Junelle has gone so quiet."

He shows me his phone screen, not a single message about table arrangements or drivers. Andrea has been so involved with planning both weddings, I'm surprised he's even still standing here talking to me and not sending strongly worded emails to the caterers or some shit.

It's not missed on me that he says he hasn't seen her in a while. Why's that? Is she a homebody? Introverted? Maybe she doesn't like Andrea, which honestly is a big fucking red flag if you ask me.

Not that I don't have my fair share of them, but any mate of mine will love my family. Our pack, our enterprise, doesn't work if we aren't all on good terms.

"I'm gonna run back to the villa. Driving or joining?" I ask, hoping I know his answer already.

"Driving. I'll help the boys get shit sorted and let Junelle have Cheyenne all to herself for a bit longer."

I nod, worried I might say something truly revealing about wanting to meet Cheyenne sooner. The night air hits my fur and I drop to all fours again, running. I have no intention of returning to the villa until everyone is safely locked in their rooms.

Cheyenne

Junelle keeps shoving the plate of toast and bacon at me at the breakfast table. Andrea is no better, scooping another helping of fresh-cut fruit onto my plate. The Italian sunshine burns through the windows of this small breakfast nook tucked away in the insane palace they are getting married in. If it weren't for the air conditioners everywhere, I'd probably be sweating buckets again like I was last night, ruining the embroidered chairs we're sitting on.

I'm exhausted, out of my comfort zone, and would really like a lightly sparkling drink down at the pier with a moment to myself. Since I arrived, it's been nonstop yapping and book signing.

I missed the fast train from Naples, and by the time I arrived at the Sorrento station, I'd missed the taxi I had pre-booked by an hour. I had quite an angry text message from the driver and a long wait at the bus stop before I could even get to the correct town. The walk up to Villa di Benetti wasn't easy either, it was all uphill. My thighs were burning and I'm sure I looked like a melted candle by the time I spoke to the security guard at the gate.

Junelle and all the aunties didn't even bat an eyelash. It was screams of excitement and so much hugging. My heart nearly burst, and I cried a little at our reunion despite how much I'd rather have a shower first. Video calls and voice notes aren't enough. For the first eighteen years of my life, I convinced myself I didn't need anyone's affection or love. My parents were cold to the point of cruelty, ruthless in their expectations, and unforgiving. It wasn't until I moved into my student housing, where I met Junelle and her parents, that I realised you could be successful and supportive.

"Cheyenne, you've gotta eat," she insists.

"I did eat something," I push back. It's true, I had several pieces of fruit and half a protein bar I had saved from yesterday.

She rolls her eyes at me, while Andrea folds his arms across his chest, crumpling his soft linen co-ord outfit. As much as I like him, I do wish he would stop trying to boss me around. We are basically the same age, and

I have watched Junelle lead him around like a dog on a leash for three years. But he's a persistent sort that you only see in romance books, if I'm honest.

I take two more bites of melon and carefully push back my chair.

"See, look, eating?" I stand up with a smile.

"Are you sure you don't want to go birdwatching?" Junelle asks.

I grimace. No, I absolutely don't want to spend the morning hiking around looking at birds. There's something about their faces, all leathery, and the way the feathers stick in their skin that makes me uncomfortable. Not that I could own a pet in my small apartment, but if I could, it would probably be a cat, an extra fluffy ginger one, ideally.

The outdoors are really not for me.

"Are you sure you two don't want to go to the pier with me?" I counter.

Andrea looks at Junelle with hope in his eyes. I know they met at the nature reserve where she works, but he's not a twitcher by any means. We both agree holidays should be spent lounging by the pool.

"We can't skip," Junelle says, wrapping her arm through his. "Plus, I know that Nonna packed a picnic that is ninety percent wine. Half the reason all the ladies go on her hikes is to get wine drunk."

Yeah, that is definitely not my vibe. Especially with people I barely know. The only person who has seen me drunk at all is Junelle. I make a face that says more than my silence.

"Okay, okay, but you're back for lunch at three so we can get our nails done," she says.

"Totally, and I will take the ride you offered down to the pier, Andrea. Just let me know how much it costs, and I'll send y'all the money."

His face goes all pinched and annoyed when I offer to pay him back. It's nice that he's so generous and caring, but it feels weird. I know it's a me problem, but I'm used to fighting for myself. If it weren't for my writing side hustle, I probably wouldn't have been able to afford this trip.

While flights and accommodation are completely covered by the bride and groom, that didn't account for the unpaid personal leave and new outfits. Being a teacher and a homebody does not make for the luxury styling of an Italian destination wedding. Also, I didn't own a single swimsuit, and at my size those aren't cheap.

"If you send me a single cent, I will sic all my aunties on you for the rest of the weekend," he threatens.

I raise my hands in a show of defeat and back away from the table. Yeah, I'm okay without that. They are a lovely group of ladies, but I have never had so many invasive questions in my life. Both of their families ask too many questions for my comfort, but Andrea's knows more about me somehow, and it's disconcerting.

Junelle squeezes my hand as I walk by, a silent understanding between us. She knows I would die for her, I would kill for her. I may not be the Gomez to her Morticia, but there is very little I wouldn't do for if she asked. She understands I'm usually a stage nine clinger or completely cut off from people.

We know each other's dark secrets, and I will forever be on her side.

Past all the opulent tiles and ornate Sicilian designs, I close the heavy wooden door to my room. Like every other room I've seen here, mine is rustic with vaulted ceilings and exposed stone walls, but one look will tell you there wasn't an expense spared in decorating it. My busted suitcase looks wrong shoved into the corner.

I heft it onto my unmade bed and rummage around for my swimsuit. After I turned thirty at the start of the year, I decided it was time to be brave and embrace my life. I shouldn't hide from myself, and I shouldn't hide from others. Following a few amazing influencers isn't going to change my mindset completely, but it made me delusionally believe I could rock bikinis for this whole vacation.

For this first venture, I dig out the lavender halter bikini. A style and colour I wouldn't normally wear, it's pricey enough I can't not wear it. The suit slides across my skin like a dream, and when I look in the mirror to adjust the ties, I *feel* good. There is a flush on my cheeks when I see the amount of pale skin I've got on display. Boobs, tummy, and stretch marks all visible without any lifting or tucking.

"You look really good, you stupid bitch." I point at my reflection. "You deserve to take up space."

The affirmation I've been saying to myself every morning makes me smile for a moment, but then I take a deep breath. Nobody is going to look at me weird or even pay attention to me. It doesn't matter what I tell myself though, my mother's nagging voice in the back of my head tells me I look ridiculous. I pull on some loose shorts and an open, oversized button-down before packing up my towel, my e-reader, and enough sunblock to paint the town pasty white.

My sandals slap against the tiles as I wander towards the foyer. The birdwatching group should have left by now, but there is a man dressed for the cover shoot of some outdoors magazine lingering by the door. His olive trousers are snug, showing off a plump ass, while his shirt is definitely hiding a well-padded torso based on how wide he is. One I bet is perfect for snuggling or grinding on with his dick buried in you.

When he turns to look at me, my entire body lights up. My cheeks heat, my heart stutters, and my clit throbs with how fucking delicious this man looks. Thank god I'm wearing a swimsuit because my bottoms are now soaked. His dark hair even turns grey and white where his facial hair begins, like he's from some kind of superhero comic.

Fuck me.

When my eyes finally drink in enough of his body, I realise he's been staring at me as well. His gaze is hot and heavy, checking me out like I'm a whole fucking buffet. Unconsciously, I wrap my open shirt up to hide myself. Shit, I'm being rude. He's dressed like he's also going birdwatching, so the group clearly hasn't left yet.

"Morning." I wave, quickly stepping up and putting on my peopling persona. "Cheyenne, I'm with the bride's side of the wedding. I got in late last night."

"I know," he says. "You don't look dressed for a hike."

Motherfucker. My lips part when I hear his voice. Wow. What would it sound like to hear him say *take my dick like a good girl*? Should I be taking notes on this guy? My fingers itch to take out my phone and start interviewing a total stranger. Like where does he get this cologne he's wearing so I can buy a bottle?

"Cheyenne?"

"Sorry, I'm supposed to be getting a ride down to Pietro's Pier. I'm not really the outdoorsy type."

"What type are you then?" He steps closer to me, but rather than move back, my feet are glued to the floor. He's practically on top of me. Every breath I take has my chest brushing against his. This unbelievably hot man dips his head lower, his fingers touching the strap of my beach bag where it digs into my shoulder.

"Um—" I don't know what to say but words tumble out of my mouth anyway. "I like being home, it's where my stuff is."

If I could kick myself, I would. That is not what you say to someone when you're at your best friend's destination wedding. You say something like museums or sightseeing. Not imply that you already want to be done with this place.

He smiles, though. Maybe I amuse him and he's humouring me for the simple fact we are attending the same wedding and staying at the same villa. Close quarters like this means you've got to play nice with people.

"Nothing wrong with being a homebody. Keeps you out of trouble," he teases.

"Oh, I'm not sure that's true." My cheeks immediately heat. Why did I say that? He's going to think I've got some sort of taboo hobby or, worse, that I'm a curtain twitcher. "I just mean that with my work,

I don't have much free time, so I like to recharge at home."

"What do you do to recharge?"

Write sex scenes that make me question my own sanity.

"Journaling, but if I need fresh air, I go to TAM. The cafe there is gorgeous."

"Can't say I spend a lot of time at the Tolson Art Museum," he admits. "But if I had a guide as gorgeous as you, I'd make a point to go every day."

I've died. Clearly, this is my own personal heaven because what do you mean this ridiculously handsome and thick man is flirting with me with such ferocity? This can't be real, but I want it to be desperately. We are standing so close together and I want him, but I don't even know his name. He's carried this whole conversation. I need to engage better, flirt back, ask him to fuck me on this side table.

"Are you with the groom?" I ask before I voice that insane idea.

"Andrea is my nephew. Valentino Benetti."

I swear to all the muses, this man is straight out of a bodice ripper. Valentino? What's next, is he going to reveal he's some kind of mafia boss or international spy? I can barely think straight when his massive hand moves to cup my cheek. The warmth of his skin is intoxicating, pulling me in closer. I step into him, letting whatever this moment, this gut-wrenching need to have his body pressed into mine, take over me.

His eyes move from mine to my lips and then back again.

"Yes," I whisper.

Valentino doesn't give the impression that he asks for permission, for anything. He takes and devours whatever he wants. But the question, even if he didn't verbalise it, makes my pussy clench. Consent is one of the sexiest things a man can focus on when he's with someone, if you ask me.

His lips are soft against mine. Gentle and hesitant when I'm expecting force. The kiss is chaste yet sets my skin on fire. Tingles shoot down my arms and right into my fingertips. This feels like fate, like worlds colliding with perfect precision to bind atoms together.

When his thumb brushes against my soft chin, tilting me up higher, he licks my bottom lip. My hands move to his shirt, tugging him closer in a quiet demand for more.

I open my mouth to deepen the kiss, and he groans. Oh my god, I'm going to come. The pure satisfaction in that sound makes my core tighten and thighs squeeze together. His tongue plunges into my mouth. Something sharp presses against my bottom lip, and I whine. This is the force I crave. I've never wanted anyone like this, with this unexplainable hunger. I want him to take me in every way possible.

He grabs hold of my waist, squeezing my chub.

No.

My blood runs cold as I break the kiss. I know he's seen me, I know that my size isn't a secret, but I can't handle anyone touching me like that, let alone the most beautiful man in all of Italy. That part of me can't ever be sexy or attractive, can it?

Tits? Sure.

Ass? Hell yeah.

The rolls of fat around my body? Surely the sort of thing that makes a man like him disgusted.

But he's still holding me, looking ready to drag me to the nearest flat surface. Valentino wants me, and I think I want to give him everything when someone starts hollering from deeper in the house.

"Tino, I gotta head up to Naples to handle…" A large guy in a sharp suit stops short when he sees the position we're in. "Am I interrupting something?"

Valentino doesn't let go of me for a beat too long. Yet another person I haven't met stares at us with a critical and creepy eye. My cheeks heat with embarrassment. I step out of Valentino's grasp, and he frowns. Yep, I've seen that look before. It's time for me to go before he makes some lame excuse.

"I should go so I can get a good lounger," I mutter at my feet.

If Valentino says something, I don't hear it. Junelle waves at me from the people carrier van, and I have enough sense to wave back and pretend like nothing is wrong. I dip into the sleek black car when a driver opens it for me. He doesn't ask where I'm going or even say a word to me, and I'm glad for it.

For the next five days, I've got to avoid Valentino Benetti or risk losing myself in him.

Valentino

L ike a light in the dark, a harvest moon shining through the smog of the city, I can't stop staring into Cheyenne's eyes. She's gorgeous in the morning light. Her red hair piled on top of her head, sunglasses nestled into it like a crown, she looks like a sleepy princess. All that beautiful skin on display. I want to bury my face in her tits and drown in them. I can't keep my distance from her when we are standing so close together.

She smells like lavender and lemons from the soap stocked here at the villa. It's subtle, complementing her natural scent. The swell of arousal that blossoms off her causes a rush of blood to fill my cock. My knot pulses at the suggestion it might actually get the privilege of being buried in her sweet cunt.

When we kiss, when she tugs me in closer by my shirt, I can't hold back the little bit of wolf that comes out of me. The growl that escapes from the back of my throat is guttural and needy. My canines extend and scrape across her plump bottom lip. If I'm not careful, I'm going to completely wolf out like a two-pump chump getting his first taste of real pussy. My hand slides into her open shirt, and the feel of her ample curves under my hand is like coming home.

But then she pulls away. She breaks the kiss, and I'm half tempted to drag her to my suite. The look on her face though, the paleness in her cheeks that were so flushed before we kissed, keeps me rooted to the spot. Did I go too far?

"Tino, I gotta head up to Naples to handle..." Luca shouts as he rounds the corner into the foyer. My underboss is dressed to intimidate and eyeing my mate too much for my liking. "Am I interrupting something?"

"I should go so I can get a good lounger," Cheyenne mumbles at her sandals. She's out the door before I can even say anything.

My lips draw back in a snarl. Luca usually means well, he's been by my side for a long time. We became made men, werewolves, together. I would trust him with my life.

"Tino, you know if you need some skirt, you can do better than… *that*. I know plenty of available females." Luca keeps talking, but my stomach curdles at the mere suggestion that Cheyenne is anything less than perfect.

Our organisation hasn't always been progressive. My father, brother, and I have spent decades beating the bad habits out of our older men and teaching our younger wolves to be respectful of all people regardless of who they are. Obviously, if you cross us, that respect is lost, but the best way to gain a following and loyalty is with mutual respect and aid.

Luca's been sliding back on some of these ideals recently.

"What's happening in Naples?" I change the subject. This trip is about Andrea and Junelle. The business with the rat following us here is frustrating but par for the course with a criminal organisation. I need to keep my situation with Cheyenne under wraps until after the ceremony. Once I've got her claimed, I'll have a chat with Luca to set him straight.

"Gio called about a lead on the head rat," he explains. "You want me to find you some higher-quality ladies on my way back?"

"No. I'm good. Get that shit sorted so we can enjoy a little vacation." I force a grin because if I don't, I'm going to punch in his fucking face. What the fuck is a high-quality woman? "How long will you be gone?"

"Overnight, maybe another day." He shrugs. "You wanna do the honours when I bring him in?"

"No, I trust you to send the right message."

I head to the door before he can say anything else to piss me off. All I want to do is make sure I give my girl the right idea about that kiss. There was something on her face before she ran off that I didn't like. It wasn't fear or disgust, it looked like shame. Nothing about what happened is anything to be upset about, except maybe that we didn't run right back to my suite to fuck like bunnies.

But there is no sign of Cheyenne, and the van taking us to the nature reserve is all loaded up. It's going to be a long day away from my mate, a long day of waiting before I can force her to explain her response. I climb in and take my seat next to Nonna.

I text the new manager of our personal pier and make sure he gives Cheyenne a good spot and she doesn't pay for a thing while she relaxes. Whatever she wants from here on out is on me. No exceptions.

"Where's Luca?" Andrea asks, leaning forward.

"Got called up for a meeting. We waiting on anyone else?" Looking around the minibus, there is only one empty seat, so I tap the driver's shoulder to get us moving. "The birds won't wait forever."

The drive up the mountain is disturbingly quiet. A few of the guys who worked the late guard rounds are sleeping, Andrea and Junelle are playing some phone game, but everyone else has some massive book in their hand. Even Nonna has one on her lap, a fancy magnifier clipped to the top of it. I lean over slightly to see what's got even my grandma so enthralled she doesn't want to tell us some story about when she and Nonno were young.

Valerie's sharp cry echoed around the empty bar. Blaze moved his hand from her breast and wrapped it around her throat. He squeezed, the rapid beat of her pulse making his dick harder.

"You like that, don't you, dirty girl?" he taunted. "The big scary biker fucking your ass raw?"

He emphasized his next thrust by biting hard on her shoulder. She nodded, tears glistening down her cheeks while her arousal dripped down her thigh. God yes, he was right. Valerie was addicted to all his roughness, all the ways Blaze took her, trying to find the bottom of her depravity.

But she'd never tell him.

Mary, Mother of God, what in the fuck is this? My cheeks heat up envisioning the scene I read. Is that what this whole book is?

Teresa, one of the many cousins on this trip, gasps behind me. Her palm is pressed against her mouth in shock. Her sister Rebecca shoves her in the shoulder and tells her to shush. I rotate more in my seat to see Nonna's younger sister, Romina, bite her nail as she reads. Is everyone on this trip but me reading porn?

"Here," Junelle whispers, sliding her e-reader over my shoulder. "You might get some ideas from this."

Andrea winks at me, his grin fucking stupid.

I click the power button, and the cover on display has a half-naked man with his jeans popped open. *His Ballerina's Secret* by Remi Roman. Sounds a little weird, but okay. I tap through the first few pages, stopping at the table of contents. Jesus, it has forty chapters.

This can't all be porn. Not that I've got a problem with what anyone reads, but when my loud family is this quiet, I want to know why. I fold my arms across my chest and get reading.

He grabbed the assailant by the throat and slammed him into the ground. If this guy thought he could attack Dante's wife, he was going to find out what happened to scum. Dante replaced his hand with his boot to hold the shit stain down before he looked at his wife.

Because that's what Paisley was to him, wasn't she? This reaction wasn't because he'd agreed to keep her stalker at bay. She was his old lady, his tiny dancer who brought a shining light into his dark life. Her happiness was all he craved anymore. Drinking and going out with the boys didn't have the same effect. A ride across the state didn't clear his head the way falling asleep in her arms did.

And this fucker tried to hurt her.

I didn't see a single bird all morning. Much to everyone's amusement, I stayed attached to the small tablet in my hand while we hiked around. Andrea and Junelle lead us up and down familiar trails while a guide points out different bird calls and nests, but I'm engrossed.

This is how I am through the picnic lunch and on the drive back to the villa. I'm so completely absorbed in this fictional world, it's only the smell of Cheyenne walking into the sitting room where all the women have congregated that I realise how late it's got. Even the handful of nail technicians with their acetone and lotions didn't faze me.

Jesus, reading can be dangerous, I guess.

"I'm sorry I'm late." She drops her beach bag by the door. "There was a huge, like, policed-off area next to the pier. Dino had to drive around it and there was traffic."

Her shirt is dry, but there is a clear area of dampness around her shorts implying she's been swimming. What do her bottoms look like? Are they lavender? Do they tie together at the sides the way her bikini top does? God, I'd unwrap her like a present on Christmas morning.

There is a red glow across her cheeks and chest from a sunburn. What I wouldn't give to be rubbing her down in aloe right now, feeling her softness give and mould to my firm hands.

From the corner of the room, Cristina clears her throat. She raises her eyebrow at me. Well shit. I look down at my hands, covered in dark grey fur and tipped with razor-sharp claws. A glance around the room shows that my capo is the only person who noticed. She gives me a thumbs up when I swipe my hand through my thicker than normal hair. No fucking ears at least. I don't think she'd ever let me live that down.

"We are just getting started, Chey, put on some dry clothes and you can pick out a colour." Junelle smiles. "Then I want the tea on the new idea you had."

I watch Cheyenne go. Every fibre of my being screams to chase her. Hunt her down and pin her to the ground so she knows not to leave a room before I say she can. Between everything that has happened this morning and the ideas this book is absolutely giving me, I need to get my woman locked down before I do something drastic like bite her throat while Junelle walks down the aisle.

My head turns in the direction of her room, and I wait until I hear the lock click shut before I stand up. Each step is like I've got concrete shoes. My feet drag across the house until I get to the kitchen. A drink should take the edge off, something to dull my senses for the afternoon. Maybe I'll sit by the pool in the fresh

air, where I won't be able to smell Cheyenne, where
no one will bother me and finish this book.

> **Dino:** About to tap out for the day.
> Nicky's taking over for me.

> **Dino:** Also Giancarlo wanted me to
> relay this to you?

> Why the fuck didn't he just text me?
> I even messaged him this morning
> personally. He's a weird guy, but
> he's loyal to the family beyond
> comparison. I guess that means the
> hierarchy of it as well.

> **Dino:** "Ciao Mr Benetti, thank you
> so much for this opportunity. We
> greatly enjoyed taking care of your
> special guest and any future guests
> you send down to our pier. It was
> a pleasure to serve her. She was
> exceptionally kind. In your message
> this morning you mentioned to place
> anything she ordered on your tab.
> Please find the receipt for the day for
> your information. It has already been
> taken care of."

A picture of a very short receipt comes through.
One slice of watermelon. That's it. Not even a glass
of water or a sandwich. Cheyenne was down there
all damn day. She must be fucking starving.

She was so red when she rushed into the house. Could she have heatstroke? My body moves while my mind races with questions. I slap together some of the leftover bits from our picnic and fill a pitcher with ice water.

> **Me:** Got it. Thanks for the update.

> **Dino:** So should I be watching this girl more closely or...

Those fucking dots hang heavy in the air. I can take care of my own mate, but I can't be everywhere. It'd probably be good to get Cheyenne adjusted to this lifestyle, to always having one of my guys with her when I'm not around. But saying all that to Dino before I've even mentioned to the rest of the family would step on too many toes.

> **Me:** No.

There, settled. I shove my phone into my pocket and start towards Cheyenne's room. If she isn't going to take proper care of herself, I sure fucking am.

I'm her mate, just as much as she is mine.

Cheyenne

I'm still in my towel when there is a hard knock on my door. *Shit, shit, shit, I need to get presentable.* The knock gets more insistent. Fuck it, nobody here will care. Junelle is marrying into a loving, but very *open* family. I won't be surprised if I see at least one random person's boob before the end of this trip. Opening the door in the oversized towel I brought from home isn't going to hurt anyone's feelings.

"Sorry, I'm coming," I call out, rushing from the bathroom to swing open the door.

Valentino looks from my sunburnt cheeks to my cleavage tan lines before he stomps into the room like he owns the place. I suppose in a roundabout way he does, since this villa belongs to Andrea's great-grandmother. But shouldn't I be annoyed that he is storming into my space like this?

"Do you need something?" I ask, holding the top of my towel up and out of the way.

"Yes," he says rather forcefully, closing the door with his foot.

He sets a pitcher and a plate of food on the fancy dresser without a single care for the wood. He pours a glass of water and hands it to me. Our fingers brush together and heat rushes through me. It's not the external warmth that has my cheeks humming like a furnace, but a deeper heat that pulses right beside my heart.

"Drink, all of it." He points at me while he says it in a very superior tone.

I've got half a mind to tell him that he can't boss me around, but I see the look in his eyes. It isn't threatening, it's not even that intimidating, but it's dark and serious in a way you only read about in books. I take the first sip under his watchful stare until thirst takes over and I chug the whole glass.

I hadn't realised I was so dehydrated after getting a bit lost in the book I was reading at the pier. It's been so long since I could just sit. Between curriculum planning, grading papers, writing deadlines during Christmas vacation, and everything else going on, there hasn't been a moment to breathe since fall break. That was over six months ago. Maybe I am burnt out.

"There you go," Valentino murmurs, stepping into my space. His thumb brushes against the corner of my mouth where some of the water spilled down my chin. "Why didn't you eat anything for lunch?"

"Uh..." I look towards the door next to me and step back. He doesn't let go of me, though. He follows me until he has me pressed against the wall. "Valentino, this isn't appropriate."

I use my sternest voice possible. It doesn't matter if I think he's stupid hot, this is red flag behaviour. It's not okay to push people around and invade their space without their consent. One kiss doesn't make it okay.

"Nah, sweetheart, I think it is, 'specially after this morning. Loving and leaving me like that," he says. His touch is so gentle on my skin, the rough calluses tickling me, but his voice is like electricity right through my veins. "I've got half a mind to put you on your back and spread those pretty thighs to see if all of you tastes sweet."

My nipples tighten. They press into the material of the towel at his words like they are at his beck and call. Humiliation sinks in my stomach and makes my clit tingle.

"Look, this morning was a mistake. I'm here for Junelle's wedding and I'm not some easy lay, if that's the impression I gave you. I'm not like that."

"Good to hear," he rumbles, voice surprisingly deep. "As for this morning, that's just the start, and I plan to make you mine by the end of this wedding."

Valentino takes a deep breath, flexing the muscles in his neck before he steps back. He raises his hand and smoothes it through his hair before he straightens his clothes like he's remembered he's got an appointment or something. I stare a little dumbfounded. What the fuck does he mean? Does he think I'm just going to be his fun hole for the holiday?

"Eat the full plate, drink another glass of water," he instructs me. "I'll let Junelle know you need a few minutes, but I want to see those pretty nails tonight wrapped around a glass of wine. Be ready to leave at eight."

I blink like a fool. I'm sorry, did I miss a whole conversation? I don't remember agreeing to go on a date. My heart is stuttering and shrieking and jumping for fucking joy, though. A man who takes initiative? Yes, please. I know the bar for real men is on the fucking floor, but this guy can't be serious.

My stomach rumbles, because of course it does. I haven't eaten enough today because I'm terrified my dress for the wedding isn't going to fit.

"Please eat, and I can't wait to see you tonight." He leans down and kisses my forehead. His lips linger on my hairline, like he's trying to breathe me in before he leaves. "I'm serious, Cheyenne."

He leaves quickly, and I fall back against the wall. Oh my god. I've got half a mind to drop this towel and pull my wand out. *I'm serious*? About what, sir? Starring in the next Tolson Times Best Sellers Romance?

I need to talk to Junelle.

My hands have been scrubbed raw, my cuticles tamed, and the most stunning shade of light purple I've ever seen painted on my stubby nails. The nail tech wasn't keen for me to skip the shaped fancy gels the rest of the group got, but once I pointed out I couldn't type with longer nails, the tone changed.

Apparently, it's imperative I can still do that.

Around me there is so much chatting and laughing, it makes my ears ring. This is for my friend, I remind myself. She is worth even an ounce of minor discomfort. I can be polite and friendly and cordial for as long as she needs me to be.

While some of the other women go outside for a smoke or vape break, others are yawning and ready for a nap. Soon it's only Junelle and me lounging in this sitting room.

Niceties first, I know surprises aren't her forté.

"How was birdwatching?" I ask, relaxing into the corner of one of the sofas.

"Good, I've got some great pictures, Andrea didn't get pooped on like he was convinced would happen," she giggles before plopping down next to me. "Look at how cute I am."

She pulls up her photos, skipping past ones of birds for me. She and Andrea are perfect. Truly, I've never seen a more beautiful couple. Every photo of them together is like seeing real love manifested. No book boyfriends could compare. Junelle looks in her element as well, decked out in hiking gear. She's always been the adventurer, willing to go where no one has before.

Even at college, field days were her favourite part of our biology classes. I was more of a labs and mathematics type of student. Junelle loves all the beautiful things the natural world has to offer. And I love praising her photography skills. It meant we made a great team for group projects, though, because presentations are my jam.

Probably for the best I became a teacher and she's working as an environmental scientist for the Harbor Island Nature Reserve. It does make field trip day my favourite day of school, though. I love getting an excuse to spend the day with her while working.

"I bet Brenda is gonna have smoke coming out of her ears when she sees your pictures." I thumb to her next photo and see Valentino in this one, his face shoved into Junelle's e-reader. "Why does he have your tablet?"

"I gave him the ballerina book to keep him occupied on the drive. Couldn't put it down." She smirks at me. "He loves Remi."

"Oh," I nod. That makes sense, I guess. It explains why he was so strange this afternoon, he knows now. Like the women in the group, Valentino knows about my side hustle. That doesn't excuse this morning's weirdness, though.

"Did you eat, by the way?" Junelle leans back and side-eyes me. Her gaze moves from the collar of my T-shirt to my calves. If we hadn't been friends for over a decade, I would have been uncomfortable with her assessing look.

"I had a few bites of your picnic leftovers. I was mostly thirsty." I make a pointed move to drink from my water glass, pinky out. "Why?"

"Tino mentioned he got some food for you, said you need a few extra minutes to eat." Her eyes narrow. "You okay?"

"I'm trying to make sure I fit into my dress for Saturday. It was a little too tight before I flew out," I confess.

"Nobody's made you feel… weird?" She waggles her fingers as she says the word weird.

Besides Valentino turning my pussy into a waterfall, the only people I've spoken to have been lovely. Even the awkward questions about inspiration were all very kind. I look Junelle over the way she did me. Nothing about her seems different from before she flew out here.

She looks the same as she did before the wedding in Jamaica, for that matter. Her brown skin is glowing with all the extra sun she's been getting, and she looks at peace. Like everything in the universe is going right the way she planned it.

"What do you mean, weird?" I counter.

She makes a show of looking to see who was outside, and if there was anyone lingering by the door. There are like thirty rooms here, all full. There is always someone just around the corner. I'm not sure who she's worried about overhearing us either.

"Has anyone tried to speak with you alone or asked you out?" she whispers.

I almost laugh and say *who here would want to ask me out*. There are hundreds more attractive people in town to take on a date. There's no way I'm the last single adult in Italy.

Except Valentino has asked me out. To dinner, no less. After I tried to suck his face off this morning after some kind of insane delirium took over me.

"Yes," I mumble. "What's the big deal?"

Junelle grabs my shoulders and shakes me before she pulls me into a hug. "This is the best wedding gift you could possibly give me. The guys and gals here are great, a little rough around the edges, but sooooo fine. Who was it? Who asked? How did they do it? When did this happen? Oh my god, was it Dino? He's very nice, not so bookish, but I'm sure he'd love Remi Roman's work."

"It wasn't Dino, OMG." I crack a smile, her enthusiasm catching. He's cute enough, but a little younger than I like potential partners. "Why is this so great? He's gonna take me out and realise how boring I am."

"Hmmm, him, a he..."

I can see the calculation happening in her head. Like Andrea at board games, Junelle can be too smart, calculating chances and counting cards. Being analytical and smart doesn't make you a cheat in my mind, but it can put the dots together a lot quicker for you. Her eyes go wide, and I swear she's going to lose her eyebrows into her hairline.

"I should have said no." I crumple into my elbow. "I'll still tell him no, that's not what this trip is about. It's weird, isn't it? Why would he even ask me?"

"There's no rhyme or reason for stuff like this," she whispers, her head bobbing up and down like there is a manual crank turning her thoughts now. "Plus, it's fine, Tino is like fifteen years older than Andrea. They act more like brothers most of the time."

"Fuck, I hadn't even thought about that," I groan.

"Babes, I've got my happy ending, you deserve yours too."

"Why are you being weird now?" Panic settles into my gut.

"Who's acting weird?" Andrea asks, a grin on his face as he sits next to us. He pulls Junelle into him for a kiss before he looks at me.

"Me, I think just too much sun today," I lie, the words slipping off my tongue so naturally. "I'm gonna have a nap, I'll see you later."

I need some quiet time to recharge anyway if I'm actually going on this date. Maybe I'll finish the food Valentino gave me and write. That always helps me clear my head.

"There's aloe in the fridge if you need it," Andrea calls, but I'm already racing to my room.

Like I wouldn't bring my own aloe vera.

Valentino

On the dot at 7:50, Junelle slides up to me in the kitchen. Andrea and most of the family are outside by the fire pit, grilling and relaxing now that the sun has set. I'm happy to see my family together like this and safe. Our life isn't one of terror, but it isn't easy either. There is always a chance an exchange will go wrong or that cops will try some stupid shit.

Or there can be a rat.

Junelle crosses her arms. *There is another beautiful member of the family.* My heart wells up with a softness I try to keep buried deep inside. For as vicious and animalistic as Andrea says I am, I've always wanted a love like theirs. When she moves, a hint of the bite on her shoulder from where Andrea placed his claim comes into view, and that softness morphs into a desire for my mate.

I could put a mark like that on Cheyenne tonight. A little wining and dining, and as much decent conversation as I can manage before I drag her out of the restaurant and fuck her full of my cum. Her shoulder would look so pretty with a crescent moon of teeth decorating it. I could kiss it every morning while we lie in bed together.

"You're dressed nice." She flicks her eyes up and down my suit. "She likes a date who is willing to put in the effort."

Well, fuck a duck. Cheyenne told Junelle, or at least enough for her to make an educated guess. She hasn't read me the riot act, at least. Maybe that's what she's going to do now, and I should try to deflect.

"Nothing is going to outshine your weekend," I promise, a smile pulling at the corner of my mouth.

"So it's like any other first date you've been on in the past three years?" She turns on me. "She's just interesting enough to warm your bed for a night?"

Anyone else would know better than to use a tone like that with me. Hell, Junelle's seen me at work. She knows what I am, what Andrea is. We don't scare her for a moment.

I still scowl at her. "Those dates were always well aware of the situation."

"Does she know *the situation*?" She pushes. Her dark eyes are discerning, like she's trying to read my thoughts before I even have them. Junelle didn't have the best introduction to our family. When Andrea said he'd found his mate, I didn't think it would be followed with *and she's in my trunk.*

"Not yet," I say before quickly pulling my soon-to-be niece into my arms. We hug for a second before she pokes my side to give her more of an answer. "But I promise, before the end of the weekend she'll know *everything.*"

She squeezes me quickly and then steps back to look up at me. "Good. Maybe you'll know everything by then too."

She smiles and walks right back out of the room. *What the fuck does that mean, Junelle?* From here, Andrea's whispered voice is crystal clear. Am I okay? More than he realises despite the current shitstorm on our hands. I check my watch and head for the foyer to wait for Cheyenne.

Prowling is in my nature, stalking and lurking just a part of the job even when you're the boss. I turn the corner but stop in my tracks when I see my girl all dressed up. My head falls back as a growl threatens to rip from my throat. Those fairy tales about wolves going after maidens are about to become so very true.

I'm not sure what this style of dress is, but the sleeves cling to her soft arms, revealing the long expanse of tan lines, sunburns, and freckles. There isn't a bra strap in sight, and the deep cut of her dress pushes her heavy breasts up in a way that has me convinced she isn't wearing a bra at all. My cock surges to life, knot beginning to fill as my canines extend along with my hair and ears.

The tight fit of her dress accents the natural curve of her body. The soft lavender gingham reminds me of lazy afternoons in the sun, sweet fruits, and wet pussy to drown in. A perfect way to enjoy my mate. She turns away from me, and the corset strings at the back of her dress pull me in like a dog on a leash.

Before I can control myself, I've got my arms wrapped around Cheyenne. I pull her plush body into mine and press my nose against her neck. Lavender, lemons, rose perfume that makes my dick twitch. I'm tempted to say we skip the date altogether and go right to my suite. Let everyone hear me claim my mate.

"I—" Her words cut off in a soft hum when I kiss her throat down to her shoulder.

"You look beautiful," I murmur. "Good enough to eat."

"I wasn't sure if this was going to be nice enough. The only other dress I brought was for the wedding. My other clothes are just like beach clothes," she rambles.

"I wasn't thinking about dates when I was packing. Junelle said this was going to be a chill trip with family, nothing fancy, but like I know that Andrea is a rich guy, and I didn't want to look weird compared to everyone else—"

"This is perfect, Cheyenne. And nobody would ever say otherwise when you're with me." My fingers brush against her stomach and her hips, the generous curves calling to me from under her frilly skirt. Her body tenses against me like it did before.

Reluctantly, I let her go with a final kiss to her shoulder. First date, meet appropriate societal expectations, then worship every square inch of her body. She turns to look at me, cheeks flushed and eyes bright.

"Do you need anything else before we head out?" I ask.

"No, I shared my location with Junelle, and I've got my phone and card in my pocket." She places her hand in the folds of her dress and flaps the fabric to show me. Not that she'll need her money tonight or ever again, but it makes me happy she's prepared. Junelle knowing where we're going is fine. I'm sure Cheyenne will take pictures too.

"Okay then, sweetheart, let's go."

Cheyenne is quiet on the drive into town. Her thighs are pressed firmly together with her hands clasped just as tightly. She nods along to her music that plays but otherwise stares out the window at the scenery. I should try to make conversation, but stealing glances at her is doing more for me. Seeing her like this, guarded and tense, tells me a lot about her.

She's nervous about our date, but her panties are still wet from when I kissed her neck. Locked in the car as we are, the air is circulating the smell of her arousal around. When we arrive at the hotel, I look over at my girl before getting out. My hand stills hers over the seatbelt.

"Are you nervous because of me or something else?" I ask.

"Being in a crowd, restaurants are loud, people might stare and judge me, what if I spill food on my dress? I barely know you, but I already feel attached to you," she confesses in a rush before swallowing as if to keep the rest of her words down.

I curl my fingers tighter around hers as warmth swells in my chest. "Trust me, I feel very attached to you already. As for the other stuff, I'm sorry I can't erase those thoughts from your head or make everything perfect, but give me ten minutes and I'll make this an easier date."

Cheyenne scrunches up her face, and it's the cutest damn thing I've ever seen. I cup her cheek and pull her in for a kiss. Her breath hitches in her throat before our lips briefly meet. She is so soft under me, so giving. I want to pull at all the parts of her until she is putty in my hands and nothing makes her feel anxious again.

I climb out of the car and walk up to the valet.

"Ciao, sir, can I have your name for the reservation?" a young man asks.

"Benetti," I say, watching the man's eyes go wide. "And we are only parking here, but I need to check something at the restaurant first. Don't let anyone near the car."

He nods quickly, and I take the short walk down the path to leave the hotel gate. The place we're going to eat has a gorgeous garden where most people dine in the same area where their food is grown. There is a historic lemon grove that the chef uses to make the best limoncello in Italy. But I also know that there is a private dining space in their wine cellar.

It's a quick conversation with the manager. The couple currently using the room to celebrate their fiftieth wedding anniversary get a beautiful, fat roll of euros from the Benettis to leave right now. When they see me standing by the front, they are quick to apologise. I also instruct the staff that my wife and I would like to dine with as much privacy as possible.

My wife. I stroll back up to the hotel with a stupid smirk on my face. She isn't married to me yet, but she might as well be. The rumour about our dining experience will surely be spread throughout the city before the end of the night.

"We are all sorted." I open her door and offer my hand.

Cheyenne takes it and blows out a breath. She doesn't let go of me either when we start to walk down the path.

"Wow," she mumbles as we walk to the restaurant. "Isn't this like sacrilegious or something?"

"Nah," I smile. "This hasn't been a church for a very long time."

I watch her every reaction as we enter. Her lips part at the warm lights that cascade from the vaulted ceilings. Her fingers clench mine tightly as she sees the garden area, the lemons hanging from the pergolas already. She doesn't notice the side glances or hear the whispers the way I do.

"Is that?"

"She must be..."

"So pretty."

The maître d'hôtel waits off to the side quietly and, once we have our fill, they lead us into the cellar. The large room has all but two sturdy chairs removed, sitting next to each other. There is already a bottle of white wine in an ice bath and a red wine next to it.

I stop Cheyenne from pulling out her chair herself. She looks at me a bit like I'm crazy, but when I do it and gesture for her to sit, she complies. With ease, I push her chair in as well and sit myself.

"The chef would like to prepare a special menu for you, Mr Benetti. Is there anything you wish not to eat?" they ask softly, pouring flavoured water from a pitcher I hadn't noticed.

"I'm happy to eat anything." I look over at Cheyenne.

"I don't like fish, but prawns are okay."

"Are you allergic to anything?"

"No," we answer together.

They nod and leave us to it. I sound like such a fucking old man when I describe our conversation like that, but that's just it. Because we've already done a background check on Cheyenne, I know the basics. She doesn't blink when I ask deeper questions. She explains why she doesn't speak to her parents anymore. I'm more than happy to listen to her rant about public education, politics, and for some reason, the economics of romance books.

"Do you read a lot?" I ask. I think I have read one other book in the last decade, but if that's something Cheyenne likes to do in her free time, I can try to get into it with her.

"Not as much as I want, but I've reached this weird point where I'm either critiquing books instead of enjoying them, or feeling bad about myself," she says.

"Why would reading make you feel bad?"

"Have you ever seen someone else's work and thought you'd never be able to compare? Like that guy in the office whose proposal is that extra bit more thorough or maybe someone is lifting just that little bit more than you at the gym?"

"No," I answer honestly. I'm not great at everything, that would be ridiculous. But I'm fucking spectacular at making sure we have the greatest people in our organisation. I was raised to never feel inadequate about anything.

"Well." She takes a sip of her wine. "I get that feeling a lot when I read."

"You shouldn't," I say with too much force. I can't make her think things or change ingrained habits with two little words. "Everyone has their own skills, and as long as you're open to learn, trying your best each day, there's no limit to what you can do."

"What podcast did you get that from?" She laughs.

"Ouch, honey." I grab my heart as if her teasing hurt me. "I happened to hear that from Zed Q talk, thank you very much."

"Do you do podcasts or anything?"

"Sadly, I was cursed with the sports gene. I'm a season ticket holder for the five pro teams in Tolson."

Cheyenne tries very hard to control her features, but she would be shit at poker. I'm not at all surprised she has no interest in professional sports. It's not exactly the most peaceful environment for relaxing.

"Don't worry, I won't drag you along to any if you don't want to."

"I like sports romance, if that counts for anything." She blushes before scooping up a dainty mouthful of risotto.

She groans as the flavours burst on her tongue. It's so damn erotic. My food might as well all be the same. I can't even remember what the previous two courses were. My cock throbs with need every time she takes a bite.

"Do you not like it?" she asks, eyeing my untouched plate.

"I'm craving something else, sweetheart." I put my napkin on the table and stand.

Before she can question me, I pull her up too. Cheyenne makes a high-pitched noise that has the wolf side of me snarling for a hunt. She's not running like prey, though. She stares at me with wide, confused eyes until I slam our mouths together. Like this morning, she melts into me.

Her hands slide up to my shoulders and her little whimper is nearly my undoing. I wind a hand around the back of her neck to keep her lips on mine while I use the other one to pull at the strings at the back of her dress. Her pulse jumps under my touch. I can't stop myself from rubbing my thumb under her soft jaw and down to the base of her neck.

God, she tastes so fucking perfect. She opens up for me, lets me lead her without a moment of hesitation when I plunge my tongue into her mouth. She groans around me, and I want to hear more of those sounds, unmuted and drawn out.

She presses her body into mine. I'm not shy about the bulge in my trousers. My dick's been hard since I first saw her in this dress, and I'm not going to settle for jerking off in the woods tonight. Cheyenne will be mine.

"Hold on to me," I instruct, chest heaving as I look down at her flushed face.

"Why?"

Even as she asks, I feel her grip on my suit jacket tighten. I let go of her neck for a moment to hold her waist firmly. Cheyenne's a big girl, soft and squishy in a way that calls to the predator in me. It's like my body knows it will find nourishment and comfort in all the parts of her she's shown me she's uncomfortable having caressed. I lift her up and set her ass on the table. She gasps as the plates rattle quietly.

"I'm going to eat my dessert now," I breathe out, doing my best to hold on to my senses. Wolfing out isn't going to get my face buried between her thick thighs. "And I want you to scream my name when you come on my face."

Cheyenne

I'm going to end up in prison for indecent exposure, but it'll be worth it to have this moment. Fuck me, Valentino can't be real. This can't be how he treats everyone on a first date. Being this accommodating but this wildly horny feels like something straight out of my imagination. I've never been one for billionaire romances, but maybe I could change my mind if they're like this.

"Is there anything you don't like?" he asks, pulling me out of my head.

He takes my face in his hand and forces me to look directly at him. Eye contact isn't something I struggle with, but I think this is to make sure I'm not lying to make him happy. His thumbs smooth over my heated cheeks as he waits for me to answer.

"Don't say hurtful things about me," I whisper.

I've been to conventions about sex education for school and for kinky book writing reasons. There is absolutely a word for this, but I'm not sure I could spell my own name right now. Valentino nods, his eyes calculating like he's trying to figure out why I don't like it.

"What do you really like, sweetheart?" He kisses my forehead after asking this time. He leads a trail of kisses from my hairline down to the base of my shoulder. His hands rest on the outside of my thighs, below the hem of my dress. My legs spread wider apart as if he isn't already notched perfectly between them. The absolute beast hiding in his trousers presses right up against my chub rub shorts.

"Having an orgasm," I sigh. Too many male partners have half-assed that job in the past, and the one girlfriend I had after college was great, perfectly wonderful, until she stole my laptop and skipped rent. Once school and writing became my life, I lost interest in trying to date again.

"Be specific," he grumbles, nipping at my shoulder.

"I like kissing, making out, a lot." With the first thing out, he starts again on his trail across my body. My breath hitches as his lips skirt over the stretch marks on my cleavage. "I have really sensitive nipples."

At my confession, he brings up one hand and tests me. His thumb brushes over the hard bud, and pleasure shoots right through my core. Even when I play with them it's not that intense. My skin erupts in goosebumps as he keeps slowly circling my nipple. My hips jerk forward against his covered cock with each stroke.

He pulls the neckline of my tight dress down until both of my carefully arranged boobs are out in the open. Valentino cups them with his large hands and still they spill out around his grasp. Anxiety rumbles in the pit of my stomach as he looks from me to my erect nipples.

"You are so beautiful," he whispers right before he wraps his lips around one and starts to suckle.

"Oh god," I whimper.

My hand flies up to his hair, but rather than pull him away to escape the intense pleasure pulsing inside of me, I hug him closer. His tongue flicks and flicks while his other hand massages my breast. He teases that nipple too, tugging at the flesh until I'm humping his lap.

He switches, giving the same torturous treatment to the other nipple. My panties, my shorts, this table are ruined. That mystical damp spot I've seen in porn and read about plenty is now a cold, hard fact in my head. I used to assume that because of my large body, it just wouldn't happen for me. My mons and labia are chubby like the rest of me, so I thought I wasn't exposing my pussy to the material for that experience.

Guess I'm wrong. Valentino blasts through whatever metaphorical dam I have, and my whole body floods with arousal. His inhale is so sharp, so strong, I wonder if he's been holding his breath when his mouth slides off my breast. He licks his lips when he looks at me, and I see the sharp points of his canines. Were they like that before?

"What else do you like? What can I call you?" He peppers me with more questions, still teasing my nipples. My brain begs me to shut off while my pussy weeps for his attention. He's so serious when he asks me this, like he's memorising and learning everything about me, like Valentino truly cares about me. I can't help but answer with the plain truth.

"I like the classics: honey, baby, sweetheart." There is a world of pet names out there. I could probably spend a lifetime researching them, but nothing makes me melt like those. I'm a simple girl with simple tastes.

He hums, kissing me again. It's all tongue and lust now. He laps at my mouth, hungrily feasting on me like I truly could be a meal for him.

"What else, baby?" he groans against my neck. "I want the kinky shit too."

My eyes flutter closed as the fear wells up. Maybe I should have taken up previous invitations to munches around Tolson to chat with kinky people in real life. Something to ease the push and pull of the feelings now at war within me. Embarrassment and excitement tug at my chest and make my clit throb.

"Soft humiliation, cum play, and power exchange," I whisper.

He growls. Like actually growls in a way that shoots a bolt of fear through me. Any sensible person would probably take that as the point to cool things off for a bit, but my body takes that fear and runs with it. It lights a blaze inside of me.

"So you want to be a little slut for me?"

"Please, Valentino," I whimper. It's needy and my knees tremble with my desire to drop right at his feet. It's a bit contradictory to like that word, but it's about the tone he put behind it. His intention isn't to hurt me, it's to call out how much I want him and for my mind to embrace what my body is screaming from the rooftops already.

I crave Valentino Benetti

"Hold this," he says quickly, pulling up the hem of my dress to my waist. He groans again when he sees my shorts. "Of course they match, so fucking precious."

He yanks them and my panties down to my ankles before he drops to his knee. Nerves bubble up. With my dress hiked up like this, he can see my stretch marks and happy trail on my belly. I haven't shaved my bush in a very long time either. The only saving grace is at least I waxed my legs for this vacation, so when he kisses my inner thigh, that part of me is smooth.

"You are so goddamn gorgeous, you know that?" He looks up at me with dilated pupils. "First moment I saw you, all sweaty in the dark, huffing and puffing, I couldn't get over you."

"What?" I can barely get the question out as he licks my pussy.

It isn't one of those cursory taste tests. Valentino buries his tongue between my pussy lips and drags it up to my clit in a long slow stroke. He wraps his arms around my thighs and spreads me wider, pinning me to the table. He tastes every part of me, licking up any arousal that clings to my skin. The rough drag of his tongue teasing my clit makes stars dot behind my eyes.

I'm so wound up, so fucking horny from his teasing I'm worried I'm going to orgasm just from this. Will he stop if I do, or will he keep going until he's had his fill of me tonight? Would he use me for his pleasure? A whimper falls from my lips when I think about him stopping because I'm too keyed up. I want the full experience if he's willing to give it to me.

"What's wrong, sweetheart?" he asks between laps of my folds. "Do you want to come?"

"Yes, but I don't want you to stop." My arms shake as I support myself.

Valentino stares at me for a moment, the apple of his cheek rising against my skin as he smirks at me. He takes another long drag of his tongue across my pussy.

"Oh, baby." His tone is a touch condescending, scratching that little part of me that I used to think was pathetic. But even thoughts like that have me squirming because, for the right partner, I am. It's so easy for me to get lost in a person who can make me feel safe to enjoy those feelings. "You aren't leaving this table until I'm done with you. This little pussy is mine, and I'm going to show her just how much I love watching her make a mess."

He buries his tongue inside me like a starved man searching for food. His nose rubs against the side of my swollen clit with each stroke. My body tenses under the sudden fullness, clinging to Valentino while he eats me out.

I moan without a fucking care in the world. Prison will be worth it for this. The pounding pleasure that pumps through me is reaching a peak. Like a coil inside me is sprung too tight, it snaps when he moans into my pussy like it's his salvation. His mouth sends glorious vibrations through my clit, and I cry out as I orgasm.

He sucks me through it, slurping up my cum while I struggle to stay upright. Finally, when my pussy relaxes again, I lean to the side and stare at Valentino. He looks downright pleased with himself, a wolfish grin on his face that makes me gulp.

"Beautiful, baby," he says with a kiss to my thigh. "But you didn't scream my name."

Valentino

This is where I want to die. On my knees with my face buried in this delicious fucking cunt and two heavy, soft thighs wrapped around my head. Cum and arousal drip down my chin, clinging to my beard in a way I hope will never wash off.

Stain me, mark me, claim me.

Whatever Cheyenne wants or needs, I'll give it to her as long as she lets me keep worshipping her pussy. The taste of her cum on my tongue has ruined my appetite for anything else tonight. Maybe one more glass of the red so she can finish dinner. My teeth are sharp, the hair on my body has grown coarser, but I don't care that I'm on the verge of shifting.

Or coming in my trousers.

Maybe this is the perfect place to wolf out. Nobody will bother us. It's only me and Cheyenne. Then I can fuck my knot deep inside her like I've wanted to for hours.

"Fuck me if you want me to scream." Her voice is so sure, almost demanding, from her relaxed position on the table. "I've got an implant, no STDs, and my last hookup was over six months ago, so I'm good to go."

I look up at my girl, and a monstrous grin forms on my lips.

"You're a dirty girl, aren't you, sweetheart?"

She licks her lips as the flush on her cheeks travels to her ears. Oh, she liked that. I slide out from between her legs and move to stand. I'm taller than I was when I first knelt, but she doesn't notice. Her fingers tremble as she grips my shirt and pulls me towards her. I'll gladly go wherever she leads me.

She licks into my mouth with a little moan. I balance one hand on the table, bones cracking as my claws scrape against the wood. With the other, I squeeze the base of Cheyenne's throat around the pulse points. It's thrumming, her heart pounding a beautiful song just for me.

"What do you like?" she asks as she pulls back. Her lips brush against mine with each breath we share.

"Domination," I growl. "I like to be in control in a relationship. I want my partner to turn to me for choices because I thrive when I'm taking care of them."

She makes a little noise, nodding along with my words. "Do you have a title?"

"I don't need one, but I'm open to talking about it later."

"Later?"

"Yeah, baby, right now I want to talk about my other kink." I slide my hand down to her tit again. Her nipples are softer now, but no less enticing. Fuck, her breasts are heavy and so perfect. I want to lie on these pillows every night after I'm done fucking my cum into her. "The one where I breed your perfect pussy."

"Oh—" She hesitates, leaning away from me. Her hackles rise at the idea, and I don't want that.

"What's that stupid meme?" I groan, trying to bring her back to me. "Marcello sent it to me a while ago with the girl getting her head patted."

"Only breed, no pregnant," Cheyenne giggles, her shoulders relaxing as quickly as they tensed up. "So some serious cum play with themed dirty talk?"

"Yeah, kids aren't something I want, but my mouth can get a mind of its own sometimes." Like when I transform and my brain moves to my knot. It's all I can think about, fucking my mate full until she's got my pup inside her belly.

"I've never looked into it," she says thoughtfully. "Maybe I should write this down."

"Why?" I ask.

"It sounds like it would be great for a book." She shrugs. "One of my characters would probably be into it."

"One of your characters?" I'm still holding her breast, but it feels like we've moved away from sex now. I move my hold to her waist. This time she doesn't flinch or stiffen when I caress her.

"I—" She snaps her mouth shut as if I'm some kind of cop. I really don't fucking like that. She can tell me anything, big or small, without judgement.

"Whatever it is, Cheyenne, you can tell me." I try to coax it out of her.

She eyes me for a moment and then her shoulders sag like she's resigned to tell me. I will find out her secrets one way or another, but seeing her defeated reaction pulls at my heartstrings.

"Sorry, I thought you knew. I'm a romance author. It's just a side hustle, but I struggle to turn off that side of me," she confesses softly. "Junelle said you read one of my books today."

My ears perk up, and momentarily I worry they actually popped out. I deal with a lot of self-important rich fucks and corrupt politicians who want their dirty secrets to stay quiet. Nobody's fame, real or otherwise, has ever interested me. I've also never cared or thought about what it would be like to meet a celebrity.

But my heart does a giddy little stutter when I realise Remi Roman is Cheyenne. A best-selling author. An author who has been on lists before based on the titles above her name on covers.

And she's demeaning those accomplishments to a side hustle.

"I don't ever want to hear you sound so dismissive of your talent or yourself again." I can't keep the snarl out of my voice. "You are fucking amazing, Cheyenne. I know we just met, and this is fucking crazy, but I am very, very interested in you and I want to be with you. Nothing's going to stop me from having you. You could tell me to go fuck myself right now, but I'll still want you, still look out for you."

"Is it wrong that doesn't scare me?" she asks.

A knock at the door stops my answer. We are definitely not fucking on this table despite how amazing that would be. Probably for the best, I'm going to end up with my knot locked in her cunt while we fall asleep. She's not scared of the intensity I'm laying out and that gives me hope. I kiss the slightly stunned expression on her lips.

"Let's get you dressed and finish this meal."

It doesn't escape me that Cheyenne finishes her glass of prosecco and then switches to sparkling water. She also eats more, like the orgasm I gave her finally opened up her appetite. Or maybe it was me hinting at how fucking obsessed I am with her. I like this, I prefer this. There is no more weird first-date shit happening. She's allowing me to see her in her nearly most relaxed state.

Would it be too pushy to have some of the boys at home move her into my house now? That's probably something to do after I claim her.

"Okay, so what do you do then? Andrea says it's some family shipping business." She looks me pointedly in the eyes. "Cause ya know… this whole thing feels like a very specific sort of *business*."

She gestures a bit wildly with her fork, a small piece of rabbit clinging to it for dear life. I love that she's asking, love what she's implying to me because it means she's not scared. Cheyenne can ask me as much about my business as she wants. But again, it's probably something that should happen after my teeth sink into the soft meat of her shoulder and we are supernaturally bound to each other.

"It's shipping, the Benettis have been in the business of moving nonperishable goods for a very long time." Since the first ships sailed from Sicily to the mainland, we've been hauling illegally traded goods to those who are happy to pay for them. Just no people, ever. "I'm the head of the North American branch of the business, based out of Tolson."

"Oh, I bet you live in that new Seaport development, don't you?"

"Right by the airport? Fuck no." I grimace. "I live near Peters Park."

"Alright Mr Fancy Pants, no need to show off to the class."

"But I like it when the teacher pays attention to me," I tease. "She's my favourite."

Cheyenne's cheeks turn an adorable shade of red. The waiter quietly knocks and then appears with a full tray of tiramisu. They cut fresh slices, place them artfully on new plates, then gently lay flecks of gold leaf on top. I've never seen the point in that shit, but she looks enthralled with it.

My girl nods and doesn't even wait for them to leave before she's digging in. Her little moan of pleasure as the cream- and espresso-soaked ladyfingers hit her tongue shoots right to my dick. Man alive, how did I get so fucking lucky?

"This might be on par with the orgasm, Valentino, not gonna lie." She grins.

I take my own bite of dessert and have to politely disagree. Nothing is better than watching her come apart.

"Do you like talking about your books or writing?" I ask. "Or is that something you'd rather talk about over breakfast?"

She opens her mouth to respond, and then I see the light in her eyes sparkle. So she likes that as well, the insinuation of more, the promise that tomorrow I'll still want her. Little does she know it's the rest of our lives. There won't be anything between us once she is truly mine.

"I don't mind talking about them to people who aren't judgy," she says. "Junelle listens to me whine about them almost every day."

"Whine?"

"I'm about to publish my final MC story for this series. It's basically all done and dusted, the date just needs to arrive. I'm supposed to be announcing a new one with this finale." She sets her elbow on the table and leans her cheek into it. "I had to force most of this last one. I'm not sure I've got any more books in me."

"Are you writing while you're here?" I ask.

"I say I am, but then I scroll on my phone for hours and do nothing," she admits.

"So maybe it's time to take a break, you've got a fancy new Italian boyfriend to hang out with." I smile cheekily. "Maybe some sightseeing can help with the burnout."

She groans loudly. "You sound like Junelle and Andrea."

I laugh. Clearly, the reason she doesn't go out and do anything is because she's working herself into the ground. That explains the little oddity in her file. After the wedding, we can get into the nitty-gritty of her work-life balance. Our trip here should only be about living.

"Do you want to go to a market or something before we head back up to the villa? Souvenirs and shit?"

"I think I'd rather see them after breakfast, if you're free," she says, wearing a hopeful, pleading look that I know is going to have me bending over backwards for her in the future.

"Let's get out of here then, sweetheart. I wanna see you out of this dress."

It's a twenty-minute drive back up to the villa. I've driven it hundreds of times before, I know every twist and road sign. Yet this is the longest it's ever been. Every traffic light sets my teeth on edge and has me barking with road rage. Cheyenne giggles at me but claims she's not going anywhere all the same. I make her put her number in my phone while we are at one stop. She sends herself a message quickly so she has mine as well, but I'll put a tracking app on her device in the morning.

Don't want to be taking any risks with my mate.

We park, and I don't miss Dino eyeing me at the gate with a smirk on his lips. That nosey little shit. While getting out to open Cheyenne's door, I send a text to the vacation family group chat for a meeting before breakfast. My phone immediately starts going off, but I put it in do-not-disturb mode.

We are not being interrupted.

Cheyenne intertwines her fingers with mine as we walk into the foyer. She looks unsure of what to do next. I hope she doesn't think I'm changing my mind because, fuck me, she is everything I need right now and for the rest of my life.

"Grab what you need to stay in my suite tonight," I say. "It's up the stairs and to the right, last door on the left."

I kiss her because I can't stop myself. And why should I? From what I can hear, most of the villa is either sleeping or doing exactly what I plan to be doing with my mate in a few minutes. My teeth drag across her bottom lip with hunger just thinking about how her thick thighs are going to feel wrapped around my waist.

But I break the kiss like a good boy. She's less interested in stopping, but when I tap her ass, Cheyenne gets moving. I watch her go, enjoying the view. I'm disgustedly excited to find out what kind of pyjamas she wears to bed. I hope they tear easily.

Cheyenne

I take another deep breath as I swipe the makeup removal wipe over my lashes. As much as I'd rather roll my whole suitcase into Valentino's suite, I'm not sure he'd appreciate that level of progression. If the orgasm he gave me is anything to go by, sex with him is going to be intense and, dare I say, magical. He says he's interested, but I shouldn't push how deep that interest goes. I need to hold on to my heart a little longer and keep the part of me desperate for romantic love hidden. I should keep this at a stage three cling for now.

One downside of thinking I'd be mostly ignored on this vacation was that I brought my favourite pj's, not my sexiest. The crop top and bleach-stained sweatpants from Old Armoury glare at me from where they rest on the closed toilet seat.

No, no, I hate sleeping without bottoms on. My thighs get all stuck together and end up irritated. I need to be honest about my comforts and likes if this is going to work out. And I like sleeping with pants on. No matter how warm it is or how hot my bed partner might be, I can't sleep naked.

I brush my hair and loosely braid it so it stays dry while I take a quick shower. Out of curiosity, I wrap my fist around the length just to see if I can, to see if maybe Valentino could if he fucked me from behind. The length of hair coils easily around my hand.

Definitely should have put a scene like that in one of my books.

I groan a little and turn on the water, trying not to think about how lost I am for ideas. Shouldn't writers always have them? I've been doing this for almost a decade, and with so many books on my backlist, maybe I've used all the words I have.

Once it's hot, I step in and let the water drown my thoughts. It stings with my fading sunburn, but I've sweated more on this vacation than I have all year. Isn't this sort of detox supposed to energise a person? In truth though, I have even less energy now that I don't have a deadline looming over me. There's no drive in my body to keep me going.

Everyone is right. I'm burnt out and this fucking sucks. I rest my head on the shower wall, a pathetic whine building in the back of my throat. Who cares if my hair gets wet now? I don't hate admitting it, but I hate accepting that I can't just go, go, go like I used to. Maybe having a new boyfriend will help inspire me.

Boyfriend.

He called himself that so it's not me rushing into it. He said it, and my heart nearly leapt out of my chest. Dinner was a whirlwind I never wanted to end, yet after he helped me put my dress back into place, I couldn't eat fast enough.

But what now? I feel locked between two revelations, one of admitting I'm exhausted from never allowing myself to rest and the other of throwing myself into a wild holiday romance that will be short-lived and leave my heart broken once I board the plane home.

The door to my room unlocks and shuts quickly.

I pause my mental descent into uncertainty and limp exhaustion, waiting for Junelle to call out. It must be her, because she knows I was on a date tonight. The hot gossip can't possibly wait till morning.

And to be fair, it's piping hot.

"I couldn't wait."

My whole body flinches, my heart jumping right into my throat while my stomach dive-bombs to my feet.

Valentino stands in my bathroom, slowly removing his clothes while he stares at me. I don't make a sound, transfixed on watching him.

He isn't a hard-muscle gym bro or even that old-school wrestler strong. His pectorals are soft, his stomach curves out in a way that tells me he enjoys life to its fullest. But he was still able to lift me onto the table at dinner. His shoulders, arms, and thighs are padded, but beneath their surface lies unbelievable strength.

For as long as I can, I avoid looking at his dick. It's going to be devastatingly beautiful, I can feel it in my gut. I want to appreciate the whole package first before I zero in on what will be the cock to end all cocks.

Valentino steps into the shower, and rather than face him, I let him press his body into mine. The weight against me is more relaxing than the hot water.

"You could've showered in my room." He smiles against my shoulder, leaving a trail of kisses across my skin. "Could've let me unlace that corset and kiss every inch of you."

"Is there something stopping you?" I counter.

It's a double-sided question, a tease on one side and a deep-rooted belief that showers make people tell the truth on the other. If he says no, there is a deliciously good chance he is going to drink from my pussy like it's the fountain of youth. If he says yes, it would prove all those things my mother used to say true. Men don't want bigger girls, and they won't pay for a cow when they get the milk for free.

Both statements are lies. My mother's poisonous language and beliefs are yet another reason I started writing romance. In fiction, the main characters put in the effort, they want to express their passions to the fullest for their love interest simply because they can. They don't follow toxic beliefs about masculinity or what relationships "should be".

They are good people.

Valentino is a good man.

"Your locked door didn't stop me from coming in, sweetheart. The only thing that will stop me from worshipping you is you." His voice rumbles as the water pounds his shoulders.

My body isn't at war over that contradicting statement. My date broke into my room, a red flag. But also he is respecting my right to say no, a green flag. I have two hands, I can hold both ideas. And a red flag has never stopped me from getting attached to someone before when a partner has done something crazy.

In fact, it's always made me a bit hotter for them. Something about actions like this makes me believe Valentino could be as obsessive as I can be. That he would go to any lengths to be with me. It's dark and twisted how much that thought turns me on, but when I press my ass back into his crotch, his hard cock is all I'm focused on.

"Let me shower, and I'll do the worshipping," I promise, reaching for the tiny hotel soap that came with the room.

"No."

He takes the soap before I can, rubbing himself across my ass while he starts to lather up his hands. I watch, because what else am I supposed to do? Valentino begins at my fingertips, massaging each little soft spot before he moves up my arm. He does the same thing to my other side. Each circle his thumb makes across my body makes my lower tummy light up.

As he reaches my shoulders, he takes his time coaxing the tension out of them. His hands work in unison to turn me to putty. I moan at one point, and he slides his right hand around my throat to pull my head back. He's gentle, careful in his caress to make sure my breathing is even without letting me move.

"I love hearing those sounds come out of your pretty mouth," he whispers. "I want to hear them every day."

Oh god. Red alert. Big red fucking alert. He can't say things like that to me. My body reacts instantly, clit humming while my knees give enough to make his grip tighten around my neck. I want to, need to, keep telling myself it's just bedroom talk, but there is a moment where we stare into each other's eyes and all I see is sincerity.

A half-hearted whimper falls past my lips.

"You like that, don't you?" he teases with a grin. "My girl is down bad, isn't she?"

I nod because if I open my mouth I will say something awful like, *never leave me*. He can't know that. Not while we aren't in the real world. Vacations exist in a liminal space where food doesn't have calories and money means nothing. The moment we are both stateside again, Valentino will see my clinginess and behaviour for the unhealthy coping mechanism it is.

"You want to know how bad I've got it?" he asks.

The hand on my shoulder slides down and under my arm until he's holding my breast. He squeezes softly. His fingers rub circles around my soft nipple until it's hard.

"Please," I whine.

"I didn't sleep last night because I couldn't stop thinking about you." He tugs at my nipple until I keen, eyes flutter closed as arousal burns through me. "I saw you arrive and knew you were mine. I had to have you."

His fingers tighten around my throat as his other hand drifts down. The soap has long washed away, but he smooths his palm across my stomach – happy trail, stretch marks, and all. I try to suck it in, anything to make myself smaller as he explores the part of me I struggle to love the most.

"Then this morning, in that fucking bikini," he groans, teeth scraping across my jaw. "I thought I was going to lose all control of myself. The only thing that distracted me all morning was a little spicy book, though lo and behold, my girl is the devious imagination behind all those scenes. She's got the brains and beauty all wrapped up in this gorgeous lavender package for me."

My body is red from the steam of the shower, but a blush stains my cheeks further with an unbearable heat that matches the one in my pussy. Is this a praise kink? Or do I just have a thing for someone as worldly and put together as Valentino seeing all that I am?

He moves my legs further apart with his foot to give him enough space to slide his hand over my mons. Two fingers spread my labia while a third glides through my arousal to spread it across my clit. My hips twitch, the sensation shooting right through me. He's already given me an orgasm tonight, yet I feel like I haven't been touched in a decade. My body opens to him without caution.

"Valentino," I stutter, pressing my hand into the tiles in front of me when he starts to play with me. His cock dips between my thighs and teases my pussy. Every little thrust he does, I move back to meet him. I want him inside me. Need it. "Fuck me, please."

"Is that what you need, sweetheart?" His voice is darker, an edge to it that wasn't there a moment ago. "Need my dick?"

"Yes," I groan, rising on my tiptoes to make the angle work.

In a rush, he turns the shower off and drags me out. I barely have time to think, but the cold drip of my hair down my back turns my brain on enough to grab the towels hanging by the door. Valentino doesn't dry me off, doesn't dry himself off, when he takes them from me. He lays them out across the bed in a haphazard and perfunctory way.

The romance writer in me is more than a little put off by the practicality of this. My face must show it because Valentino chuckles. He cups both of my cheeks and kisses me. The heat is still there. His tongue delves into my mouth and teases mine until my fingernails are racking down his back.

"I want you on all fours, ass up, so I can watch your pretty pussy swallow my cock," he says, lips bumping against mine. "Is that okay?"

"Yes," I say a little too eagerly. The pounding, hips-slapping roughness that comes with taking a dick from behind makes my brain turn off. It's a surefire way to make me cock drunk. It won't necessarily lead to an orgasm though, and I want that. "Can I use my vibe?"

"Knew it was a good idea to break into your room. Yeah, grab it, baby."

I dig it out of my suitcase. I know you can't actually feel when a person is watching you, but my pussy feels Valentino's eyes on my ass when I bend over. When I turn around, he's lazily stroking and squeezing the base of his cock, a hungry look in his eyes.

"I'll have that." He takes the vibrating wand from me with his other hand. "Now, on your hands and knees."

There is something not just revealing, but incredibly awkward about climbing onto a bed still dripping wet while a partner watches. Not seeing him either makes me suddenly more self-conscious, but then I turn my head to see him grab two of the pillows from the top of the bed. He folds one in half and slides it under me at my hips.

"Drop so your face is on the bed, sweetheart," he instructs, and I follow instantly. "How's this feel?"

He presses his hips into my ass, the head of his cock teasing my clit. The pillow keeps me propped up and nestled at the perfect height. Then he falls forward. Valentino traps me in this position with his lips pressed against my throat, hot breath tickling my skin. His fingers entwine with mine and he stretches us forward.

Oh fuck.

"Do you need more support?"

Yes. Yes, oh my god. I need a fucking intervention before I do something crazy like profess my love for someone I met this morning. I've never had a partner provide this much attention to detail while also taking such a controlling role before. He grinds against me, waiting for me to answer.

"This is good," I squeak when his tip teases my hole.

"That's my girl."

He kisses along my neck as he slides back to stand behind me. A chill rushes down my spine at the loss of heat. Valentino squeezes my hips and ass, spreading my cheeks wider. I flush under his inspection, but his groan makes it all worth it. The sound reverberates through my body right to my pussy.

"How do you feel about edging?" he asks as he presses a finger slowly into me.

"Not tried it," I gasp. "Prefer coming a lot when I touch myself."

He hums and fucks his finger into me slowly. For as rushed as we were to get into bed, he takes his time working me up. He eases a second finger into me carefully, like I'm not dripping arousal across him and the towels beneath us.

When his hand leaves my hip, I know what he's doing. The sound of my wand turning on mixes with the wet sound of his fingers inside of me, and I shudder. My pussy clenches tight with anticipation.

"I'm going to tease you, but I want you to tell me when you're close, baby. I don't want you to finish until I say."

"Why do you wanna torture me?" I tease.

Valentino chuckles but doesn't answer. He presses the vibe onto my clit and my complaint crumbles. My body shakes and my fingers curl into the sheets as the imaginary coil in my core turns tighter. The wet sound of my pussy brings me higher and higher.

"Stop," I whimper, as my core starts to tighten too much.

"Good girl." Valentino takes the vibrator off my clit and removes his fingers. I groan at the emptiness. Unable to come, I can't keep myself from squirming. He bites my ass and I want to wail. "One more time, and then I'll fuck this perfect cunt."

His fingers slide into me with ease and start pumping. I clench around them instantly. I'm already so close now my body hums with need. When Valentino curls his fingers down, they brush against my G-spot. I gasp loudly as it lights me up.

"Yes," I moan. "Yes, right there."

"Your pussy is gripping my fingers like a vise, baby," he growls. "So fucking beautiful. I can't wait to have my cock buried right here and feel you come."

The vibrator touches my clit, and my hand shoots back to signal for him to stop. I can't get the words out as I nearly orgasm from the light pressure. Valentino moves quickly at my trembling hand. One second his fingers are inside of me and the next the tip of his cock is pushing into my pussy.

I choke as he bottoms out. His dick stretches me to my limit. He is so deep inside me I feel it in my throat. Unable to talk, to beg for more, to scream to the heavens about the godly cock they've gifted me. Valentino grips my hips, and the pinpoints of pain where his nails dig into my skin cause stars to form behind my eyes.

"Your pussy," he sighs. "Fits me so well, sweetheart. Fucking made to take my cock."

He leans forward, bracing one forearm near my head. My eyes roll back at the shift in position. I'm not going to survive this. Every part of me tingles with the potential of us and what we're doing. My heart pounds a rhythm in my chest that makes me believe in fate. That Valentino and I are meant to be together.

"Now be a good girl and let me breed this pussy."

There aren't words to describe what that does to me. I can't explain how something that has never interested me before takes root in my brain and overwhelms me. The need to have Valentino's cum coating my insides and keeping it inside of me is primal.

He fucks me hard, with a determination that has me believing he will breed me. I gasp and moan with every slap of our bodies together. His presence over me grows and grows until it feels like I'm drowning in him. He overwhelms all parts of me. Every breath we share, every brush of our skin, sends me higher and higher. Am I going to come just from penetration?

"Fuck, Cheyenne, you're taking me so well, squeezing me," he groans, pressing his lips into my shoulder. "Like you want me to fill your cunt with my baby. Is that what you want?"

"Yes," I say without any thought. "I need it."

"You're gonna get it, sweetheart. If it doesn't work tonight, I'll fuck you full again in the morning, and every day after that. Any chance you'll have me, I'm going to bury my dick in your pussy until your belly is round and your tits are swollen with milk."

Every word is gruff, heated and growly with tension that lines Valentino's body. I'm a mess, ruining the pillow he's tucked under me and surely the towel too. All the thoughts running through my brain are going through the same filter. They are screaming for me to orgasm and take every drop of cum he can give me. My mind only sees our completion as life-saving at this point.

"When you come, I want you to scream my name."

It's the only warning I get before my vibrator is pressed to my clit. My body short-circuits, every limb shakes as the tight coil of arousal in my lower belly twists to the point of breaking. I can't feel anything, but the buzz of my toy working with the girth of Valentino's cock stretching me impossibly wider. Every stroke feels like he's getting bigger and bigger, thrusting harder into my pussy.

There is a rush of pain when he buries himself a final time and starts rocking against me instead of pulling out again. The power of it mixed with the vibration on my clit makes my world explode. I scream for Valentino, my voice cracking as my words descend into a shout.

"That's my good girl. That's my mate," he snarls in my ear.

He kisses my throat again, and then my world turns white. Sounds and feelings disappear. All I know is that my body is sinking into warmth and euphoria. I'm not sure how long I bask in the nothingness of it, but Valentino's slow, deliberate kisses on my shoulder and neck raise me up. His cock twitches inside of me, but he doesn't pull out.

I'm at a loss for words. I should get up and go pee, clean up a little, but as Valentino rubs his hand down my side and hips, I can't think of anywhere else

I'd rather be. There's no quaking sensation when he touches the pudgy parts of me. The world is quiet. It's only the two of us and we've got nowhere to be.

For now, I let the anxiety of what could be drift away and focus on our connection.

On the magic of us.

Valentino

Cheyenne snores.

It's like an adorable little boat motor has cuddled into my side. But instead of a blade tearing my shins to pieces, it's icy toes.

I couldn't be happier.

After my knot finally deflated and my cock slipped free, I took a bit of time to get us ready for bed. Between the bucket of cum leaking from her pussy and the blood on her shoulder, it probably would have been easier to shower again. Cheyenne didn't so much as stir though when I got out of bed, and I didn't want to disrupt her sleep.

Plus, no reason to alarm her about the half-sealed mating bond on her shoulder. That can wait until she wakes up and it's all healed. A few warm washcloths later she was cleaned up. I tossed the bloody, torn towel into the bin and the cum-soaked one into the bathroom.

Then she rolled into my side the moment I got us under the covers.

I haven't slept this well in years. Not because of any sort of qualms about my life choices necessarily, but there is a sense of fulfilment and wholeness with my mate in my arms at last. The morning light begins to peek through the heavy curtains, but I don't want to get up yet. My claiming mark on her shoulder has healed completely, another sign she is my mate if the instant need for her wasn't enough.

Her heart beats with mine now, strong and steady. The closer we're together, the clearer our physical connection will be. Dad always said he could sense from a mile away if Mom was coming home spitting mad or happy as a lamb. Andrea and Junelle are the same, they can read the other's emotions based on physical reactions. It was funny at the start of their relationship watching them fumble through it.

No doubt we'll have our moments to look back on and laugh at too.

Cheyenne does a little huff in her sleep when I finally extract myself. I pull on my clothes haphazardly, stopping every few moments to kiss her mark, her forehead, her cheek. I can't fucking stop myself. I'm too damn happy.

Once I'm out of her room, I pull out my phone. Sure enough, my family is my family, and there are a double-digit number of messages. While most I give a cursory glance, I do read a few.

Andrea: do we even need this meeting?

Dino: can I start having meetings when I get laid?

Junelle: I'm putting all of you on a sex ban.

Cristina: agreed. I need my fucking beauty sleep

Marcello: we should really upgrade the soundproofing

Ugo: I've already cut off my ears

Andrea: not your special ears D:

Marcello: but who will listen to my beautiful singing now?

Ugo: bonus :D

Cristina: me next

Junelle: me three pls

Me: Gimme 15 and I'll see you all in the dining room. Someone make sure Nonna has her coffee.

I see most of these smug fuckers in the hallway on my way to my suite, but not everyone is as vocal as those five. Plus, there is the fact that everyone at home will need to be informed, but that can wait until we are stateside again. Mating Cheyenne now has led to more admin than I was expecting, but I suppose I'm not missing the introductions back home. Seeing a new business associate or other mafia syndicate and being able to introduce her as my mate will be a treat I savour until my dying breath.

A quick shower and a fresh set of clothes later, I'm taking my seat at the head of the dining table. Nonna wraps her dressing gown tightly around her shoulders, as if it isn't hotter than sin, and takes slow sips of her cappuccino while we wait for a few of the men from security to come in. All in all, we squeeze about forty-six people in here.

Besides myself and our matriarch at the opposite end, Marcello, Cristina, Ugo, and Andrea sit at the table. The chair to my right is empty for Luca, though he's still in Naples. The others also remain empty for the capos and enforcers we left in charge at home.

Junelle leans against the back of Andrea's chair with a tired but very hopeful look in her eye. I have no intention of following a sex ban, but maybe for the sake of the bride I'll move my plans for Cheyenne tonight to my suite so we are further away.

I wonder if she's ever worn a gag before.

"As you're all mostly aware of what happened last night, I want to confirm that Cheyenne and I are now mated."

A short round of congratulations and hugging wakes everyone up slightly. For the wolves in the family, they aren't too surprised, but for the human partners in attendance, this is fresh and exciting news.

"Is it too early for limoncello and prosecco?" someone asks.

"Yes," I say quickly. "Cheyenne doesn't know the full extent of what she's been brought into, so please just continue as you were."

"But with earplugs," Marcello jokes.

There is a good-natured laugh around the table, but my eye connects with Nonna. She smiles into her drink but doesn't say anything. I'll take her subtle approval over the cheering congratulations any day.

A stirring sensation in my chest forces me up and out of my chair. I don't even bother saying goodbye or see you later. The wolf rises in me, directing me to go to my mate immediately.

I have enough sense not to return empty-handed and grab the first thing I can from the kitchen before I'm practically running down the hall. My shoes crack against the tile as the stirring turns to a dull ache.

What in the fuck is happening?

I hear the shower running before I'm even in the room. It doesn't stop me from bursting through the door. I drop everything and, without thinking, step into the shower where Cheyenne is crying.

She jumps, and the spike of her fear makes me flatten my proverbial ears and tuck my tail. I wrap my arms around her and pull her into my chest.

"What's wrong, sweetheart? What the hell happened?" I demand.

"It's stupid," she says with a sob. "I'm just PMSing or something. Please don't think I'm crazy."

"Tell me." I bite back a growl. She's not hurt, there's no one to kill, but I'm struggling to stay in control and human.

Cheyenne pulls back and looks me in the eye. It's been a morning of looks and staring contests. I need words.

"Tell. Me." My hand curls around the back of her neck and I squeeze.

"I woke up alone and felt shitty. I know we joked about breakfast, but it just…" Her bottom lip trembles again. "Stupid, I know."

Every fibre of my being wants to wolf out. I want to expose every secret I have to reassure my mate that she won't ever be truly alone again. That she will never be without me. The mark on her shoulder is barely visible, she probably doesn't know it's there, but I do. Soon she'll understand the importance of it.

I settle for a kiss. One that is hot and claiming as I try to convey how much I feel for her. Cheyenne moans into my mouth, and I have half a mind to drop to my knees right here and show her where I want to spend my every waking moment.

"Oh my god, your clothes," she suddenly gasps and pushes on me. "Did you even drop your phone?"

"No." I smile. "Because all that mattered to me after my morning meeting was getting back to my girl. And it seemed like you needed my reassurance."

I don't give a fuck if my entire wardrobe goes up in flames right now. Cheyenne turns off the shower and starts removing my clothes. My cock takes a keen interest in this turn of events. Her hands smooth over my chest hair, and when she drops to her knees, I nearly croak.

"Fuck, you look good down there," I groan.

She scrunches her eyebrows together and then looks at the hard outline of my dick in these linen trousers. Summer suits are essential for staying cool, but fuck can they make a man's ego grow. The look on Cheyenne's face nearly has me blowing my load.

Be polite, tell her to ignore it or something. She doesn't need to do anything she isn't up for.

"What I wouldn't give to see those pretty lips wrapped around me," I say instead, cupping her cheek.

"Tell me." She half smiles, using my own two words against me now.

"You trying to bribe me, honey?"

"No, I'm just curious. What do you think a blow job from me would cost?" She pulls my soaked phone from my pocket and slides it away from all the wet. That thing is fucked, but I'll get Marcello to put my SIM into a burner. "Me sucking your dick is for my pleasure."

"Dirty girl," I mutter.

She peels my pants down, cock bobbing up and down with how hard it is. Cheyenne swallows the head, tongue teasing the underside. She closes her eyes as she starts to work my dick. I can't take my eyes off her. She's so fucking gorgeous and all mine.

"At least a fifty-k allowance, a portion of my house, and my undying loyalty."

I start listing off all the things I plan to give her once we are back in Tolson. With each new gift or shared interest, she sucks a little more. Every date idea I come up with, she sucks me down harder. When she gags, her throat constricts around my cock, and heat builds too quickly in my balls and at the base of my spine.

"Baby," I pant, the scent of her arousal overwhelming me, "I'm gonna come."

She doesn't slow down or pull back. My knot is swollen and throbbing. Thank fuck she's not looking at me. Her hands find leverage on my ass, and she gives me a hard squeeze that practically surprises the orgasm out of me. Shocks shoot through me and out my dick as Cheyenne swallows every drop of my cum.

My knot deflates quickly without the pressure of my mate's pussy keeping it warm and sensitive. She pulls back as a final spurt of cum lands on her cheek.

"How much fruit do you eat?" She giggles and swipes her finger over her cheek, popping it into her mouth. My eyes practically roll back. "I've never actually enjoyed swallowing before."

"I eat enough." But it helps that we're supernaturally matched and mated.

Is this heaven? It feels like it. My chest is warm and fuzzy, but I can't tell if it's her or me. Oh my god, what will it feel like when we next have sex? What will it feel like when Cheyenne orgasms?

My dick twitches at the idea of making my mate come. But not in the shower. Somewhere soft she can relax and luxuriate.

"My turn."

I pick Cheyenne up bridal style, and her squeal makes me laugh.

"Put me down, holy shit."

"You're fine, sweetheart. You weigh basically nothing," I grin, curling her in my arms.

I've always been a strong guy, and after getting made, my strength increased unbelievably. So many broken doors in my twenties is a small price to pay to make my girl feel weightless.

"This is so unreal, I don't think I've ever been picked up."

"Well, get used to it because I like having you in my arms."

As I put us into bed again, Cheyenne grabs whatever it is I thought would work for breakfast and laughs. She shakes a bag of Goccioli, and while I suppose those are a breakfast item, they're not exactly filling after our loud night.

"Alright, here's what's gonna happen. You're gonna lie back while I eat your pussy, and then we're gonna get dressed and do tourist stuff for the rest of the day."

"What about the wedding plans? We can't skip." Cheyenne runs her fingers through my wet hair, scratching my head lightly. I get why dogs kick their leg now. Fuck me, does that feel good.

"No plans today. Andrea and Junelle are so busy with the final planning we've got the day to ourselves," I reassure her with a kiss.

One that starts my quest down her luscious body to salvation itself. I lick and suck on her clit until she's begging me to stop and her cum has soaked my facial hair.

Euphoria wraps us tighter and tighter in its embrace.

It's surprisingly overcast for late April, the sea bringing a cool breeze with it. We barely make it outside before I'm running back to grab one of the two sweaters I packed for the trip. It's warm in Italy, but the weather at home has been chaotically cold.

Cheyenne gives me a sceptical look but then pulls it on when I don't make a move to open the car door for her. It fits, baggy around her arms and shoulder, but a stretch around her hips. She rolls it up so it's tucked around her waist above her shorts. It's a perfect compromise. Like this, I can slide my hand over the little sliver of skin showing whenever I want so I can feel her, skin to skin.

Again, I use the hotel parking lot. The streets are less crowded today. The unusual weather keeps most of the tourists at bay, while at the bus stop a crowd of them wait for the shuttle to drive them the ninety minutes to Pompeii. We walk the pavement hand in hand as I guide Cheyenne through the streets. I spent most of my summers here, learning how to pickpocket, scam tourists, and anything else my grandfather thought me and my brother would need to know to run the family business.

I point out little nooks with centuries-old statues, and Cheyenne demands we take pictures together at every one. We stop into little souvenir shops, the small backpack she brought slowly filling up with meloncello, lemon-themed homeware, and enough hard candy to give all of Tolson a cavity. All the while, I listen to my girl. She ums and ahs at everything we see, tells me how she and Junelle met at school, and lets me see a city I view as my second home with new eyes.

Everything is exciting and fresh, and for the day I'm just a normal guy.

But the feeling doesn't last.

Outside of Bonamico, a gelateria that's been serving what I consider the best ice cream since my nonna was a kid, I get a call from Luca.

"Order whatever you want," I smile, handing over my card for her to pay. "And get me the Vinder Buena flavour."

"Sounds good." She salutes me and walks into the shop.

I give her another moment, watching her step into the queue, before I answer the phone.

"Hey, Tino," Luca says quickly, "we've got a problem."

My tongue rolls over my flat teeth as I step further away from the store. I round a corner into a narrow alley to get some semblance of privacy.

"What's going on?"

"I don't think we are looking for one guy anymore. There's someone else working with him in the organisation."

"You have any leads?" I push.

"Not yet. I've put my feelers out with Marcello's regular crew, but I'm still digging."

"Alright." I rub my brow, wiping some of the sweat away. "What time are you back? Andrea's stressing is gonna boil over if you aren't back for dinner tomorrow night."

Luca better damn well be back at the villa for dinner. Both the bride and groom will ride his ass into next week if he doesn't show. Andrea has been stressed enough about making sure we've got all the family together for this, he'll be crushed if Luca misses any more of vacation.

I sense the hesitation in his silence, though. My second isn't going to be back tonight.

"You can fucking call him and tell him, just know I ain't around today to smooth things over."

"What the fuck do you mean you aren't around?"

"My *mate* and I are busy being tourists." I grin.

"The chubby girl from yesterday?" he asks, the disgust in his voice evident.

"Watch your fucking mouth," I growl at his tone. Anger rises in me like a fucking geyser about to burst. "Cheyenne is mine, claimed and all. You put some fucking respect in your voice when you are speaking about her."

"Sure, boss. I gotta go." He hangs up without another word.

How fucking dare he? That's fucking it with him. We're having a meeting first thing after the wedding. I shove my phone into my pocket. God-fucking-damn it. What the hell is wrong with him?

I walk back onto the main street just as Cheyenne is stepping out with our cones. She looks around, but it's clear she can't see me as a throng of tourists pushes between us and the tour guide shouts about the history of gelato. I'm already shoving through them when I hear it.

The sound of a knife cutting through a bag, of Cheyenne's gasp, of a tussle.

A lanky man with blond hair has one hand on the cut straps of my mate's backpack and the other raised to fight her for it.

I explode.

I don't wolf out, I'm a grown fucking man, but I don't hide who I am either. My fist collides with his face, and he stumbles to the ground. One kick to the gut stops him from trying to get up, and a second to his face has him gushing blood from his nose and mouth. I wrap my fist around his T-shirt, squishing ice cream through my fingers.

"Who the fuck do you think you are?" I snarl, shaking the guy. It doesn't matter that I used to do the same shit. I'm too amped up, the need to care for and protect my mate overriding any sense of decency I have. "Do you know who I am?"

"Get the fuck off me!" he shouts in Italian, scrambling to kick at my shins.

"Do you know what it means to cross the Benetti family?" I counter back in our mother tongue, seething with rage. "That's my fucking wife you raised a hand to. I should gut you right fucking here."

He blanches, just like I knew he would. Around us a crowd is forming, all the eyes and cameras are bad for business, I know. I know. But I want to make this man suffer enough to remind the local gangs who owns these streets. Before I kill him for even looking at my mate.

"Valentino," Cheyenne's quiet and urgent calling pulls me back though. "Valentino, the crowd."

Motherfuckers. Fucking hate all these goddamned smartphones. I shake the guy once more and toss him into the street. From behind us, David, owner of the gelateria, steps out and quickly ushers us back inside the now empty store. He's a quiet man, but a good one. He hands me a damp towel to clean my hands, while Cheyenne's shaking fingers tug at a loose piece of her hair.

"Did you throw your gelato at that guy?" I ask, trying to distract her. Shit, she looks like she's about to freak out.

"Yours too," she whispers. "Gut instinct."

"Have a seat in the back and I'll bring you something fresh," David says, walking behind the counter.

I guide Cheyenne, snagging two bottles of water from the fridge on the way. She sits, crossing one leg over the other. A blush rises on her cheeks while heat blossoms in my loins. It's impossible to resist. I take a deep breath disguised as a heavy sigh.

There it is. She's turned on. Did seeing me get in a little fight make her pussy wet? What about it triggered this response from her? I was ready to beg for her understanding before we got back here, but now I'm wondering if we need to skip gelato altogether.

"You okay?" I ask, struggling to keep what I know a secret. She hums a little, so I press her more. An unabashed smirk forms on my lips. "You look a little flushed."

She looks towards the counter where David has his back to us, watching the door. "That was... hot. I've never seen someone get punched in real life, and you looked so aggressive and you did that for *me*."

The way she says the last part stirs something in me. A sort of sadness that makes me wonder what people haven't done for Cheyenne before. My physical reaction to this news affects her almost instantly, the slight droop in her posture obvious to me. We will definitely be having our gelato.

"That is the least I could do for you, sweetheart," I promise, taking hold of her hand. "There is nothing I wouldn't do for you."

Cheyenne

The rest of our day is a blur of tourism, aching feet, and an amount of introspection I wasn't planning on when I accepted my invitation to this wedding.

The gelato guy gives me a plastic bag to put my souvenirs in while Valentino takes me on a trek to find his favourite leather goods guy. He seems to know everyone as we're walking around. Shop owners wave or nod when they make eye contact with him. The manager of the handbag store nearly refused to let him pay for a new backpack for me. I didn't even try to pay after I saw the price tag. Valentino's his own man with his own fancy money. If he wants to spend it on me, I'm happy to let him.

"How do you know who everyone is?" I ask as we're leaving the store.

Valentino leads me down another winding alleyway, his finger wrapped tightly around mine. "I used to spend summers here when I was a kid. My parents wanted to make sure I was properly Italian."

"Versus what?"

"Versus being a guy who can't speak a lick of the language, doesn't know there's more to our food culture than Sunday sauce, doesn't know his family history."

The way he says family history catches in my thoughts. He's clearly got something going on deeper than what he's shared with me so far. I guess the question is whether or not I'm okay with that. He looked ready to beat my attempted mugger to a pulp earlier. If I hadn't said anything, I'm sure we'd be in a fucking jail cell right now for manslaughter, or whatever the Italian equivalent is. There wasn't an ounce of care in his body about hurting someone who'd tried to rob me.

Valentino would have killed that guy if I hadn't reminded him of the crowd.

The way I could feel his anger, his fury and disdain somehow palpable between us made me want him to do that too. I wanted Valentino to hurt that man irreparably for trying to steal my bag.

And it turned me on. My pussy soaked my panties so fast I was barely holding it together while we ate our gelato. What does that say about me? I've always been able to draw the line between fantasy and reality. My parents, for as shit as they were, drilled into me what was good and bad behaviour in their eyes. It caused me to repress a lot of shit, but I know the way I felt shouldn't be right.

It shouldn't matter why he was doing it, Valentino has shown me he has a violent side. I should be running for the hills. Instead, I wanted to crawl into his lap and ride him into the sunset. No one has ever fought for me, especially physically. Junelle is accepting and supportive, but I would never ask for anything more. I wouldn't have ever asked anyone to do what Valentino did for me, but I keep replaying the scene in my head.

The way my bag began to slide off my back, my phone in one hand and two ice creams in my other while I tried to find Valentino. The rough tug, the shocked reaction of throwing our ice cream, the frozen response when the guy raised his fist at me. Then the clap of knuckles meeting cheek. He stood over that total stranger, fire in his eyes, and I think that's the moment I will tell people I knew Valentino was the guy for me.

Years from now, when people ask me how I knew I'd found the one, it will be this moment. My man was ready to commit murder in broad daylight for me.

And I only stopped him because of the crowd.

Valentino

I'm walking on the spiritual plane. Clearly, all my bad deeds haven't landed me in hell, but in heaven. That's the only way to explain how I've got so fucking lucky with Cheyenne. My passionate little homebody who likes it when I beat the shit out of a stranger. Who let me buy her things all day and do my fair share of rambling about spots I used to loiter around and cause trouble as a kid.

It's been a day I never want to forget, even with our little hiccup.

This is like the sweetest cherry on top of a perfect day.

The bonfire crackles in front of us as we settle in for the night. The whole family lounges outside, feet up and staring at the sky. We don't get this back in

Tolson. Between work and all the trappings of being an adult, we don't get to take too many breaks. There is always someone who needs to talk to us, someone who needs something or wants something from us. This little destination wedding is the closest thing to a vacation I've had in years.

On my right, Andrea gazes at the stars, his fingers tapping on his thigh like he's trying to count them. Cheyenne's curled up on my other side, facing Junelle and whispering about some drama that I don't really understand. They laugh and drink, and I bask in the pure, unadulterated joy coming off my mate.

It's almost easy to forget there's a rat, forget there is business that will need my attention soon. As much as I'm on vacation, I'm still the boss. I've still got a capo imprisoned who needs to be released. While our lawyer is working on it, I've got to make a call tonight to grease the wheels. I want my man out. It's been months.

But a few more minutes won't hurt.

"You've got to apply for this one. Their form just opened." Junelle's bright phone light blinds me as she turns in my direction.

"Cons are a lot of work. And what if I run into someone I know from school? People will want to take pictures with me and blegh," Cheyenne says.

"What con?" Andrea asks.

Embarrassment coats her cheeks and my heart heats with it through the bond as Cheyenne looks over her shoulder. I can't help but smile. I don't remember the last time I've felt anything remotely close to this.

"You've got to trust people more." Junelle passes her phone to Andrea. "This is a big deal book signing, you could meet readers who have been following you for years."

"How many people would be there?" I ask. "What are the details?"

"It doesn't ma—"

"Seduced in Tolson," Andrea shouts over Cheyenne. "July next year, open to all romance genres, two days of signing, expected crowd of two thousand excited readers, at the Zarro Opera House Convention Center."

"Please, Chey, give me something to look forward to," Junelle whines.

Andrea gapes at his fiance's antics, but my mate still doesn't look sold on the event. I grab the phone and look at the basic sign-up form. It's not overly revealing, the company that's running the event is literally called *Seducing in...*, and while I could have my guys back home do a full deep dive into them, I don't want to force my girl to do something she isn't ready for, or that could be dangerous.

She's done an amazing job of protecting her privacy from the average citizen, why ruin that anonymity now?

"Baby, you'd be a shoo-in, but if you don't want to go, I'll find a reason for us to be away that weekend. And any other weekend you need me to," I promise.

"They're just a lot of work," she whispers. "I'm already exhausted thinking about it."

"That's the beauty of having us as your assistants, though." Junelle throws her arm over Cheyenne's shoulder. "You know we could make it work for you."

Cheyenne looks at Junelle, then back at me. I'm not going to tell her no or yes here. This is her choice, her career. Whatever she decides, I'll support her.

"Send me the link, and I'll think about it," she says.

"That's what I'm talking about." Andrea smiles. "You know if you do, we'll all be there as the Remi Roman cheer squad."

"Oh, we could get shirts," Junelle exclaims.

"And I will be here to fight off these yahoos if you don't want to," I assure her.

Cheyenne nods before she yawns. "I'm going to head to bed, I think. What are the plans for tomorrow again?"

"We've rented out the pier for the day for some private swimming, then family dinner in the evening. Nice and easy before the big day," Junelle says.

"Sounds good." She yawns again. "See you in the morning."

I stand quickly and offer Cheyenne my hand. Her soft fingers slide over my palm, shooting warmth through my chest. *My mate.* We walk back to her room, and just as I'm about to open the door, my phone vibrates in my pocket. She raises her eyebrows at me when I don't immediately answer.

"Go ahead, but don't lock the door."

"And if I do?" she teases, a little sparkle in her eyes.

"Then I'll break in, and you'll have to see how I punish dirty girls who don't listen." A growl rises in my throat, the predator in me hungry for a chase.

"Don't threaten me with a good time, Valentino."

Cheyenne opens her door and disappears, leaving the door unlocked. I like this side of her, all playful and relaxed. I want to do everything I can to keep her this way. A smile still plays on my lips as I answer my phone.

"Talk to me."

"Mr Benetti, how are you?" Rick Mooney, the city mayor, greets me.

"I'd be better if you weren't falsely imprisoning my friends, Mooney." I keep the smile on my face even as he sputters down the line.

"The DA has a very solid case against di Carlo. They found everything the tip said they would. His computer has everything they need to put him away."

Shit.

I pinch my brow trying to think who in our fucking family would plant evidence against Ezio. He's an old-school guy, even if he is younger than me. He's too damn smart for his own good and knows that he can't leave a digital trail. He still does all our *other* accounts on physical books because he doesn't trust the government not to be watching him.

On top of everything else, for us, not being able to shift fucks with our mental state. It makes us volatile, weakens our mind until we break. A werewolf can only remain sane in captivity for so long before they snap and tear apart whoever comes near them.

So who the fuck has that sort of information and hatred for us, while also having Ezio's trust? Every person I can think of, I immediately dismiss because they wouldn't double-cross us like that. If we were simply human, I could let the paranoia take hold of me.

We are wolves, though. We are a family and a pack. A secret beyond the laws of man binds us together. It's something that shouldn't ever be corruptible.

"You should be grateful it doesn't implicate the rest of the Benettis."

"Are you trying to say something?" I growl.

"No," he nearly shouts. "No, no, of course not, Mr Benetti. I'm simply saying that it's interesting the laptop only threw one of your men under the bus."

Yeah, the one man who makes sure our money is safe and accounted for. No money means no business, which means our clientele start looking elsewhere for secure shipping. This fucking rat is trying to cut us out completely. Systematically taking us apart and using any associate who is weak enough to fall for his alpha bullshit.

"Have you ever heard of a computer growing legs?" I ask.

There's a pause on the line. Mooney's not a smart man. He wouldn't even be fucking mayor if weren't for me, but really, I'm asking a pretty obvious fucking question here. He needs to hold up his end of the bargain and help us out when we ask him to.

"I've heard it could happen," he whispers like a fucking weirdo.

"What happens if this one does?"

"I suppose with the right judge, they could be persuaded to lighten the sentence to probation seeing as he's been locked up for a few months now… assuming said computer pays his rent."

I grind my teeth together. This greedy shit stain. We are not allowing him to be re-elected. On principle, I don't work with the pigs. They are nothing short of scum of the earth. But fuck, would it be useful sometimes to plant one of my people in their building as a cleaner or something so they can just take the fucking thing out of lock-up.

"You're pushing your luck, Mooney. Do you not remember exactly how you got your shiny new office?"

There is a pause on his end, and then he clicks his tongue. "Of course not, Mr Benetti, the people voted for me."

He hangs up and I stare at my phone. What in the fuck is going on? Did I miss a message? Am I actually dead and my ghost means jackshit to people these days? Mooney has never had a backbone before, and I don't believe this reaction is coming from nowhere.

This rat needs to be got rid of now before I start losing my mind. Luca claims he's got a lead, so I need to trust he can handle it. Even if his attitude has been off recently. Once he meets Cheyenne and we work through whatever's got into him, it will all sort itself out.

I need a drink.

The kitchen is bright when I round the corner. Dino and Ugo eat leftover risotto right out of the dish, not even stopping as I pull a glass down from the cabinet. It isn't until I have a second glass of grappa that either of them speaks to me.

"That bad, boss?" Ugo asks around a mouthful of food. He looks down at the cold rice in an offering, but I shake my head. I only want the burn of liquor right now.

"Call your guy, Dino." I breathe heavily around another shot, begging the alcohol to dampen my spirits before I wolf out and put a fist through the wall. "I want Mooney smeared from the North Side all the way down to Kingston. Anything but us is on the table. I want it over every fucking tabloid and gossip site."

"Can do." He smirks.

"What can I do?" Ugo's grin is downright fucking crazy. He smells the blood in the water and wants his turn. He's a hungry wolf, and he hasn't been fed in a while.

"Once we are home, once Ezio's back at our table, I want you to make that stupid fuck suffer."

I take a third shot, the burn in my throat doing nothing to stop how out of control I suddenly feel. It's a drink meant to be enjoyed, and I've practically wasted it just to have my edges sanded a little softer. I want to rip out Mooney's stupid fucking tongue, but I can't do that right now.

"You alright?" her soft voice calls from the wide entryway. Cheyenne's got her phone in one hand, her arms crossed over her chest to hide her tits from anyone's view. She's dressed for bed but done waiting for me to come to her this time.

Worry, concern, and a deep sense of care trek across the planes of my chest as I look at my mate. She feels all those things for me. It's almost suffocating how much emotion she's packing through our new bond, but all I want is to be smothered in it right now. I want to hear her voice and have it drown out all the worry sitting on my shoulder.

"We've had a long-time client break contract," I say, words chosen carefully to avoid lying. I don't want to be dishonest around her. She can know as much or as little about my day-to-day life as she wants, but I need to ease her into it one secret at a time.

"What a dick bag," she states simply. Her words already have a smile pulling at my lips, reminding me that Mooney is nothing for me to really stress over. He's just a bag of dicks I need to take out to the trash.

"He wishes he was that useful," Ugo snorts. "More like a cum rag someone forgot under their bed years ago."

Cheyenne's nose scrunches up as she walks towards me. Her pretty eyes are heavy with the need to sleep, but she leans against the counter instead. Her free hand rests on my back before she slowly starts rubbing up and down until I could almost feel the ghost of my tail fucking wagging.

"Was it a bad break?" she asks.

"I don't tolerate disrespect," I answer. "And nobody ices me out of business."

Her head cocks to the side. The loose braid of her hair falls off her shoulder, and I take the chance to grab the wispy tail of it. I smooth my thumb over it like that will soothe me.

"If there is no legal recourse, then I guess you could get creative. Maybe he can be scared straight." Even as she says the words, I'm not sure she believes them. Nor do I think she truly understands I'm going to scare Mooney to death.

"How would you ruin a fictional man from one of your books?"

Her cheeks colour at how blatantly I'm talking about her writing in front of others, but I'm genuinely curious. She's a creative, devious little author. There must be a multitude of ideas running through her head about how to make a person suffer.

"Depends on what he did." She eyes the boys, but they look ready to take fucking notes. "I had one guy rip out another guy's fingernails one by one. I don't know if that's really doable though."

"With the right leverage," Ugo says. He scratches his forehead. "And long enough nails."

"Any other ideas?" I press.

She purses her lips while she taps a blunt nail on the counter. "Oh, I saw in an episode of this vampire show once where a guy had his guts spilled, but they purposefully kept him alive so he had to see it. The effects were gnarly."

If only I had more surgical precision. Ugo, however, has perked up immensely, abandoning the cold food in front of him to lean across the counter to talk to my mate.

"What's the wildest way you can think of to torture a man?" he asks.

I pull up a barstool for my mate, and I listen to her and Ugo brainstorm torture and murder plans. My mate doesn't know it yet, but she's downright perfect for our family.

As long as the werewolf thing doesn't terrify her.

Cheyenne

I wake up with a mouth between my legs.

Valentino holds my thighs close to his head, using one of them as a pillow as he lazily kisses along my labia. My breath catches in my throat as his nose bumps against my clit. This is a completely new experience for me, and it might have unlocked a new kink.

"Morning, baby," he murmurs, voice still rough with sleep. "Couldn't stop myself from getting a taste of you."

All I can muster is a small, affirmative noise. A blush spreads across my face as I think about how long he could have been down there. Was it seconds? Or has Valentino been slowly coaxing the arousal out of me? My body thrums with pleasure, with a soft burning need that makes me think he's been sipping me like a fine wine.

"Is this okay?" He pushes up on his elbow until he can meet my gaze. There isn't a hint of teasing or a smirk on his lips. He's checking in on my boundaries, because even though this wasn't a hard limit for me two days ago when we had a fast rundown of kinks, I could have changed my mind.

How wrong that assumption is though.

"S'good," I swallow. "Please don't stop."

He groans, diving back between my legs with vigour. My fingers curl into the sheet beneath me as he flicks my clit with his tongue. I want more, I want to feel Valentino on top of me again and drown in his body heat. My muscles wake up, tensing and flexing, as my need to climax builds quickly.

"More," I whimper.

"So greedy in the morning." His heated breath makes my skin tingle.

A solitary finger slips inside me like dipping an ice cream cone in hot fudge. Valentino slowly strokes the wall of my pussy with slick ease. His tongue scrapes over my clit and my back arches. This isn't enough to snap the coil tightening in my lower belly.

It just makes me squirm.

"Valentino," I huff. "Fuck me."

He pushes a second finger into me as a response. Those two fingers stretch me, but they don't make me as full as his cock did. This isn't anything compared to the stretch of his shaft, the pulsing heat from it. I want that, damn it.

"If you don't put your dick in me" – I grab hold of his hair – "I will find someone who will."

He snarls, like my words have awoken a beast inside of him. Before I can even take my next breath, he cages me in. His body pins me to the bed, the crushing weight of him trapping me with my legs spread wide open. He holds still over me, just far enough so my eyes don't cross when I look into the burning heat of his.

"Who owns this pussy?" he demands, harsh breaths fanning across my face. His cock hovers in front of my entrance. I flex my hips, trying to fuck myself, but he doesn't let me. "Answer the question, sweetheart."

"Me. Now fuck me."

I wrap my legs around his waist, but he moves at just the right time. He thrusts and angles himself so the tip of his cock presses against my clit. I groan in frustration.

"We can do this all morning, Cheyenne. Hell, I could spend all day teasing you and we can just skip a nice day at the pier."

He knows what he's doing. I won't miss time with Junelle. But I need his dick inside me. I'm not sure what has come over me, but I can't bring myself to taunt him. The words float through my mind, but not past my lips. They part and nothing comes out because I need him to fill me. I need his cum inside of me again.

"Who owns this pussy?" he asks again. He shifts his hold, gripping one of my thighs and pressing it higher. His cock head slides across my clit and notches at the opening of my cunt.

"You do," I whimper. "You, Valentino, just please fuck me."

"That's right." He spears into me, all the way to the base of his dick. He moans into my mouth, not kissing me, just teasing me as I gasp for air. He punctuates his next statement with hard snaps of his hips. "This slutty little cunt is mine now."

Thrust.

"Mine to lick."

Thrust.

"Mine to fuck."

Thrust.

"Mine to breed."

Pleasure ripples through me, growing into a wave of ecstasy as he starts to fuck me seriously. He unleashes himself on me, grunting and groaning until I'm not sure they are even human noises. My short nails scratch his back and slide down his sweat-slick skin.

"Shit, that's it, baby, mark me."

I dig in harder, not even worried about if it hurts because it makes him fuck me faster. His pelvis slams against mine each time he bottoms out, heavy sac beating my ass as my body starts to fold in on itself. He pushes me up until my hips are raised above my head and blood starts rushing to my face.

"You want my cum, don't you?" he asks. All I can do is nod. "That's my dirty girl. Such a slut for me."

"Only you," I choke out. My chest aches as I say the words. It's just for him. I've never let myself feel as much as I do for another partner this way. I've never admitted to liking these things to another person. It's all for him.

"Fuck," he moans. "Just what I want to hear, baby. So damn good for me. My perfect mate."

Valentino squeezes his hand between us and starts strumming my clit. With all the blood in my body rushing to my head, I'm not sure I hear him right, but I don't care. He called me perfect. My body sings under that praise, and I let go.

My orgasm crashes over me, leaving me gasping for air. I stare at him the whole time, his tanned skin, thick beard, and beautiful brown eyes all mesmerising as my pussy convulses around his cock. He fucks me until I'm trembling with aftershocks.

"Gotta make it stick," he grunts.

He rubs fast circles around my clit, bringing me right to the edge of another climax. It happens so quickly, my legs shaking with the sheer force of his hips pounding into me as he pinches my sensitive nub.

"Valentino," I squeal as my second orgasm blindsides me.

He slams into me, pulling back just a little as his dick swells and starts to flex with his own orgasm. He makes a noise in the back of his throat like a wounded animal. I wrap my limp body around him the best I can, running my hands up and down his body to soothe him.

I don't know what that sound means, but I want him to feel good just like I do. We collapse sideways, his dick slipping out of my abused cunt. Cum smears across my thighs, but it's not what I'm worried about now.

"Are you okay?" I ask, pushing his hair away from his forehead. It's so thick, I'd probably be jealous if he hadn't just fucked my brains out.

"I'm dead," he groans. "But I died the happiest I've ever been. Tell my family I tolerate them."

A hoarse, weaving laugh bubbles up out of me. Valentino buries his face in my boobs and sighs while I continue to pet him. He holds me tight, cuddling and caressing my body with pure reverence. He doesn't seem at all ready to start the day or leave the bed. I can't say I blame him. Right here in his arms is where I'd happily stay for the rest of my life.

"Are you okay?" he asks after a few minutes.

"Why wouldn't I be?"

"I'm just checking in, sweetheart, seeing how we're doing on the comedown after a bit of rough sex." He kisses the side of my breast before he nuzzles back into me.

"I'll take this kind of wake-up call over my alarm any day," I say. "Even if I do have a sore vagina now."

He lifts his head quickly. "Is there anything I can do? Run us a bath or—"

A sharp knock on the door cuts him off.

"Sex ban," Andrea shouts. "Some of us are trying to remain innocent before breakfast."

My cheeks heat.

"Fuck off," Valentino hollers back.

"Fifteen minutes," Andrea says before he stomps away from our door like a child.

Valentino laughs against me, his shaking body making me jiggle along with him. He doesn't let me go. Instead, he grips my ass and pulls me closer to him until we are fused from top to tail.

"Are we banned from sex now because I was too loud?" I ask, ready to crawl into a hole and die.

"He's just being annoying. I want you screaming for me. We can always try a gag if you're nervous about it, though."

He wags his eyebrows at me, and I can't say I'm not curious. How loud would he make me scream then?

But we only have fifteen minutes to get ready now. I'm not going to be late even if I'm embarrassed. I kiss Valentino, tasting myself on his lips.

"Let's get dressed."

"You know the meme of like a stick figure rabidly tearing apart something?"

"Uh." Junelle looks up from her e-reader and stares at me. I only just see her movement out of the corner of my eye because I can't stop staring at Valentino as he steps onto the pier.

His wet swim trunks, already so seductively short, are skintight. They cling to his thighs and outline his heavy dick. I can't take my eyes off him. Every drop of water that slips down his skin makes me jealous. I want to be those rivulets.

This certainly lightens my mood after he stormed off to take a work call.

After we all got set up on the pier, loungers unfolded and umbrellas opened, he had to take another call. I'm starting to notice a trend with Valentino. He never seems to turn off his work brain either. I guess the one benefit for me is that I don't have to deal with people breathing down the phone at me.

Thankfully, this one wasn't nearly as long as last night's, but he spent a good thirty minutes pacing up and down the far side of the deck.

Whatever it was clearly didn't make him happy. He stripped out of his loose button-down at the end of the pier and climbed right into the water to go bother Marcello and Cristina where they were swimming. They all wore serious looks and then the two of them left.

Junelle didn't bat an eye.

I only watched them pack up quickly for a few moments before I saw Valentino getting out of the water closer to us.

"I'm turning into a feral animal, Junelle."

"We all heard." She laughs, looking from me to Valentino, then back at me. A satisfied, victorious grin settles on her lips.

I groan and shove my face in my paperback. Definitely going to have to learn to be quiet.

"The Benetti men sure do have a way about them," she agrees. "We clearly hit the hottie jackpot."

Her gaze shifts just enough, and I see Andrea walking towards us. Unlike his uncle, he's cut with obvious bulging muscles from all the time he spends doing… something. He's not a gym bro, so maybe his corporate job isn't as white collar as I thought. He's got to get those muscles from somewhere, right?

"One green smoothie." Andrea smiles as he presents Junelle her drink. "Marcello said he'd be back before dinner."

"Where'd they go?" I probe.

"Eh, apparently Nonna thought she saw a rat." He shrugs overly much.

My blood runs cold. Nope. Big no. I can't deal with mice or rats or any rodents. I know there is some statistic that when you live in a big city you're always within five feet of one, but I can't believe it. Even thinking about it makes it feel like they're scratching and crawling all over my skin.

"What's going on?" Valentino asks, picking up my legs to sit on my lounger. He puts my feet back on his lap and starts rubbing up and down my calves. The action calms me slightly, but I still feel a chill rake down my spine at the thought of rats.

"Don't want to talk about gross rodents," I say quickly, scratching at my arm. "Just anything else."

The three of them exchange looks.

"Did you put on enough sun cream?" Valentino asks.

He's moving before I can say I slathered myself in it. Andrea and Junelle start talking about the DJ for the wedding, but I'm struggling to focus. Valentino *moves* me. Like really moves me. Like I'm a coffee mug on a desk who just needs to be scooted an inch to the left so it doesn't spill on graded papers. He squeezes in behind me on the lounger, pressing his wet body against my dry one.

Well, one part of me isn't dry.

"Don't worry about the rat." He squirts cream, the smell of sunblock wafting up over the smell of seawater. "He's a problem for me to handle."

"Didn't know exterminator was in your job description," I joke.

"All a part of the job as the big boss."

He's so serious when he says it. I'm really not sure how to respond and thankfully I don't have to. His big hands smooth across the open back of my swimsuit.

I thought this one-piece would be more appropriate for today, seeing as this is a whole family gathering thing, but Valentino barely touches the straps and they are slipping off my shoulders. He massages cream across my freckled skin, pressing his thumbs gently into my muscles. My body melts under his firm touch, and my eyes roll back as he rubs away the knots in my shoulders.

I bite my lip to keep from moaning.

Sex ban. Sex ban. I will not show weakness in front of Junelle and Andrea. I'm stronger than the pulsing heat growing between my legs as Valentino sneaks his finger into my suit to ghost across my breasts. I just stare at my book, only to realise these two fictional idiots are mid fuck as well.

I'm absolutely going to fail.

"Is the water cold?" I ask, voice strained and squeaking.

It wasn't two days ago. I know it's the perfect temperature. We just need to get away from my best friend before I make a fool of myself. We've been through so much together, but I can't be this horny in front of Junelle. There has to be a limit, right?

"No, it feels really good. You need to cool off, baby?" Valentino's lips brush across my ear as he speaks. As he leans into me, his hard dick pushes against my low back.

He is doing this on purpose.

"Join me." I don't ask. If he really wants to tease and play games in public, he'll follow me.

The first step into the water makes goosebumps erupt across my skin. Valentino is right there with me, waiting his turn to climb down the ladder. It's better to take the plunge and get adjusted quickly, so I leap the rest of the way into the water. Coolness rushes across my heated skin, but the desire rippling through my core is still there, hot and heady as I break the surface of the salty water again.

I wade around the pier, smiling at his family as they play in the shallower waters. One of his cousins, I think, points at her float to ask if I want it, but I shake my head. With a little effort, I swim further out. At the far end of the pier, there are large rock formations to keep the waves at bay. There are no posted rules about swimming past that point, so I'm hoping we can have some privacy just on the other side.

Valentino follows me without question until I'm pulling myself up onto a flat rock. He gives me a boost when I get one leg up.

"Cooler now?" he asks, a cheeky little smirk on his lips. He spreads my thighs until he can stand between them.

"You're such a tease."

"I don't know what you're talking about." He feigns innocence. "I was simply helping the most beautiful woman on the pier protect her skin."

"Uh-huh, and your dick was helping you how?" I smooth a hand through his wet hair, slicking back his black locks until he looks like he actually might be a mob boss. A smile plays on my lips. Now that's a thought. A mafia man always makes for a hot love interest.

"Keep petting me like this and we'll see just how helpful he can be," Valentino says, leaning further into my touch.

"Are you getting nervous about tomorrow?" I ask, changing the subject.

"What's there to be nervous about? It's going to be a great day."

The way he says that hits me a bit oddly. Like his defences are up for something that I thought would lighten the mood. Of course, tomorrow is going to be awesome. Junelle has been keeping her dress a secret and I can't wait to see it. I also know the menu for dinner looks like it will be to die for.

Assuming my dress still fits.

"Are you giving a speech or anything?"

"Yeah, Andrea said if I didn't, he'd have the boys destroy my house," he scoffs.

"The boys?"

"Just friends back home," he says quickly. "Speaking of which, what are your plans when we get back?"

Butterflies erupt in my stomach. I try to school my features, to keep the smile on my face soft, but I'm barely containing myself. "Why you asking?"

"I know a spot, and I wanna take you to it." He kisses my leg, dragging his teeth across my inner thigh.

"What kind of spot?" I breathe heavily.

"One of my favourites, has the second-best view in Tolson." Valentino's so close to my pussy now, the heat of his breath making me ache for him. "After the view of you in my bed."

"Who says I'm going to be in your bed?"

It's just a tease, a playful little taunt, but just like this morning, a growl rips through Valentino. His hands wrap tighter around me and drag me to the edge of the rock. It cuts into my ass but puts me at the perfect angle for his face.

"I think you need a little reminder, dirty girl, that you belong to me. This ain't just some vacation fling, this is the start of you and me." He pulls my swimsuit to the side, revealing my wet pussy. My heart pounds in my chest as his words circle around me like a spell, bringing out all the feelings I try so hard to keep tamped down. "*Nothing* is going to keep me from you. You are mine, *forever*."

Those words stick with me through every kiss and orgasm he gives me on that rock. *Forever, forever and ever.* Every possessive thought I've ever written into a book has manifested into this man, and I'm falling for it. He's all those red flags, and the obsession lurking in the depths of his eyes makes my heart ache for more. He drinks from my body until I'm too weak to swim back to the pier.

But he carries me, holds me tight as we lounge in the shade of the umbrella, feeds me little pieces of fruit until the sun starts to set. There isn't a moment today when I am not surrounded by Valentino Benetti.

It's not until dinner at the villa, seeing everyone surrounding the table and laughing like one big happy family, that I wonder if this could really be my new life. I'm wearing the same dress from our first date, the gingham having the exact same effect on Valentino tonight. He can't keep his hands to himself. It reminds me of how Andrea was when I first met him. It had been so blatantly obvious he was obsessed with Junelle that I nearly wrote a whole book about them.

Is that what's happening to me now?

Valentino and I are seated right next to each other, and I know that wasn't the original plan based on the empty setting nearer the middle of the table. Rather than being closer to Junelle, I'm seated right next to the head of the table like this is actually some kind of mafia-type shit. This isn't *The Sopranos* though, right?

Right?

Based on everything I know, based on everything I have seen these past few days, based on Valentino, I can't stop thinking that maybe "shipping" isn't their only business. It's not like I could find Andrea on ConnectIn when I first met him.

Junelle would tell me though. She wouldn't keep a secret like that from me. It might not be something she could outright say, but I think she'd drop hints for me to put the pieces together.

If this were something dangerous, she wouldn't put me in harm's way. Just like I would never do that to her either. I can't stop the panic though that I'm in over my head all of a sudden. The weight of this trip, of everything with Valentino, comes rushing back to me. All those years of learning to hold myself back are now colliding with the realisation that I might actually be falling for a mafia boss.

"You alright, sweetheart?" Valentino asks in a hushed tone as dessert is cleared away.

Am I? Shouldn't I feel bad for the thoughts that have been volleying in my head? Shouldn't I be scared that I'm growing attached to a man clearly capable of immense violence?

Fuck it, I'm not growing attached. I am at full-on level nine clinging. He would have killed for me after barely knowing me. Valentino has seen all that I am, listened to my boring stories about work and writing, and still he can't keep his eyes off me. He wants to keep me near him now and forever.

"Would you ever hurt me? Even if I upset you?" I ask softly. My gut says no. The moment the words are out of my mouth, disgust roils in my belly. The room around us grows quiet and tense, but I keep staring at Valentino, watching his facial features. Would he lie to me?

"I would never let anyone, myself included, live for raising a hand to you."

"The man the other day is still alive," I argue, trying to point out the absurdity in that statement because a normal person doesn't talk like this.

"For now," he hedges around an answer before going back to my original question. "But no matter what, we will solve our disputes with words and respect. How I am with the outside world has nothing to do with how I am with my family or with you, Cheyenne. Do you trust me?"

His emotions are written across his face. Valentino is scared.

All this time, I thought I was the one who would grow too attached too quickly. That my clinginess would turn him off. But if anything, he needs me to spell it out for him. Just like I would do anything for Junelle, I would do anything for Valentino. He still has his secrets. He could be a serial killer, but my head and heart are aligned.

"With my life." I smile.

He leans into me, and I meet him halfway. Our lips brush together chastely, and I only draw away because I know there are eyes on us. Junelle winks at me when I look her way, and my cheeks heat. Andrea looks fucking smug before he raises his glass in the air.

"To family, and to love," he shouts.

The table erupts with cheers. We down our drinks and that's that. Our holiday is nearly over, the wedding is tomorrow, and it seems I'm going home with more than just some souvenirs on Sunday. This short time away has been more fulfilling than I could have imagined.

"Grab some of your things and stay in my suite tonight," Valentino says. "I've got a surprise for you."

"Is the surprise more breaking and entering?"

"No." He kisses my forehead. "I'll be waiting."

Despite that promise, I lock my door anyway. I'm not risking him barging in on me using the bathroom. That's a bridge we can cross later. I strip and put on my pyjamas. Unlike the other night, there is a level of security and confidence I feel wearing them now. If anything, when I look in the mirror to remove my makeup and say my words of affirmation, I believe them with my whole chest.

"You look really good." I smile at my reflection, a wine and excitement-fuelled flush on my cheeks. "You deserve to take up space."

I stuff my earbuds into my pocket, and my toothbrush and a few other toiletries into my makeup bag. Time to get my back blown out for the second time today and see what sort of surprise Valentino claims to have for me. We've barely spent any time apart, so I doubt it's a gift. But maybe he's going to spill what he's been holding back from me.

If he tells me he runs a criminal organisation, I'm absolutely going to barge into Junelle's room and cry at her for not telling me.

I flick off my bathroom lights, horny imaginings twirling around my thoughts. There's a shift in the sudden darkness. My heart jumps into my throat and my skin prickles. It's probably my imagination, a little too much sun mixing with the prosecco at dinner. I turn the light back on and there's nothing.

"If you're a murderer, you have to tell me," I joke to myself in hopes it clears up the uneasiness in my stomach.

Obviously nobody responds, and I turn the light off again. The room is bathed in darkness with a faint glow from outside. My eyes adjust as I slide on my sandals to make the walk across the villa.

Then something moves out of the corner of my eye. A flicker of red light, maybe the AC unit is switching functions. That's the logical explanation that my brain is trying to feed my overactive nervous system. Like a chilly wind coming up from the harbour, a shiver tracks down my spine all the same.

But then I hear it. A pair of knuckles crack, or maybe it's someone's back because the sound gets louder and deeper until it's a cacophony in the dark. Then there is silence again. It's almost worse, my heart rate climbing as my throat tightens.

Clack.

I can't breathe.

Clack.

I can't move.

Clack.

The sound of thick, sharp claws dragging against the tiles makes my blood run cold. What the fuck is going on? What is in my room? I'm too scared to even lift my phone. My makeup bag is crushed to my chest with trembling fingers.

Heat radiates from the shadow towering over me as it wraps a claw-tipped hand around my throat. Glowing red eyes look at me with such disdain, such hatred, I didn't even know was possible for a monster.

We stare at each other for a moment before his grip tightens. Was he hoping I'd scream? I can't move, I can barely fucking comprehend what's before me. My cheeks bulge as I try to draw in a breath.

It's only when he lifts me off the ground that my body does anything. I drop my phone and bag, grabbing his wrists for leverage to keep him from crushing my windpipe. His fur is thick and coarse, my useless nails unable to do any damage. Everything starts to burn as my vision blurs and my legs shake.

"I'm worse."

Just as I think I might pass out, he turns and raises me higher until I'm dangling over his massive form. His outline becomes more obvious. Like 'out of some B movie, a white werewolf materialises under the moon before I black out.

I wake with a fright, coughing and sputtering. Visions of a white wolf cloud my thoughts for a moment, but then I hear regular human voices. Nothing supernatural is happening here. My brain was just working too hard earlier.

"She's awake," one man says.

"Leave her in the cage for a bit longer, disgusting slut."

I flinch at the response. That man's voice sounds familiar. It tickles something at the back of my head, like I've heard it recently. The sound of a podcast turning up a little higher stops any possible memory, some dudes complaining about how modern media is infecting men with femininity.

When I swallow, my throat hurts. The rest of me aches from whatever else has happened, but when I rub my ankles together, I'm still in my sweatpants. My hands are tied behind my back, but not tightly. Like they don't think I'll try to get out of here. My head is wrapped in some sort of scarf. It tastes like silk or satin when I lick it. Something about the slinky material is nice around my face, but every screech of a chair reminds me that this isn't a fun time.

This is a fucking nightmare.

I've been kidnapped.

A chill rushes down my spine.

I've written scenes like this before. Dark romance is something that I've found comfort in, a safe place to explore the desires I've had since I realised what sex was. For years, dreams of being kidnapped and held as a sexy captive have titillated me because I never thought anyone would care enough about me to go to such extreme measures. My intensity around relationships, the way I cling onto people, has always been risky. Coming up with excuses for friends who used me in high school, to bed partners who were terrified at how I felt about them.

Valentino's the only person who's been able to meet me stride for stride that way.

Obviously, I realise this is a crime. And this is not how I would want my dream abduction to go. For one, my imaginary stalker isn't here. They don't listen to shitty podcasts. They know I don't like to be humiliated that way, too. Fuck, even Valentino understood that when I said it to him, but this man isn't trying to turn me on. He's trying to scare the shit out of me. I really should be taking this more seriously.

Maybe making some mental notes will help. If I can assess the situation better, I can decide what their plan is for me. Given the security around the villa, I don't think this is a casual pick or even a response from the pickpocket the other day. This was not an opportunistic snatch and grab. I also know that of the demographics for kidnapping in Europe, my body type doesn't usually fit the bill. There are exceptions to everything of course, but I'm hopeful this isn't a sex trafficking situation either.

I twist my wrists until I can pull one hand through the loose ties. My fingers smooth over the material, it's not nylon rope or really rope of any kind. From the raw, fraying edge, I think it might be a torn shirt or sheet. They could have torn up my bedding to use as a last-minute binding. Underneath me is a cheap, padded cushion based on how it squishes under my fingers.

They said I'm in a cage. What size is it? I slide my feet around slowly until I can find each of the edges. It's not very big. My legs are still bent, and I barely have to stretch to touch both corners. I have a choice now. My hands are free. Do I stay like this, or do I pull off my blindfold? It's a risk, and I probably shouldn't do anything to upset the guys who took me, but if they are going to be bad at their jobs, that's not my fault.

Quietly, and sending out a prayer to every deity I know, I slide the silken scarf down until it covers my throat. My eyes flutter as they adjust to the light. We are in some sort of warehouse office. There are a few empty desks, a large window looking out into the open – based on the glow of the morning sunlight warming the room – and two men sitting on computer chairs watching a video recording of a podcast.

"And let's not forget our sponsor for today's show, SupraNutrients. Let me tell you, this shit's amazing. I put a scoop of their MaxMan protein powder in my morning protein shake before I hit the gym every day. My hair is thicker, my dick game is better if that's even possible, and I swear on my life, guys, it brings the high-quality ladies right to my door. The testosterone coursing through me is at 110%. This absolutely works and will make you the alpha male you want to be."

I think I'm going to throw up.

There is enough space for me to sit up in the cage. This is more like a kennel for one of those massive security-type dogs. That poor pup is hopefully on duty if I'm taking up their house. I think that might break me more than anything if I found out they hurt a dog. Hurting an innocent pet should put you in one of those horrible bottom rings of Dante's Inferno.

"What's taking him so long, Luca? I thought you said he actually gave two shits about the fattie. We've been here for hours," the man on the right complains.

Hours? Hours! Do I have a concussion? After a strangulation, victims usually wake up in a few seconds to a couple of minutes. It's long enough to be tied up, but not much else. I rack my brain for what could have happened. I don't feel woozy or nauseous, my throat fucking hurts, and I imagine my face looks a bit roughed up. Did I hallucinate the werewolf?

"Tino won't rush in, even if he can find us," Luca says. He looks back at me, and I recognise him as the creep from my first morning at the villa. Our eyes meet, his flicker red and I swear his light blond hair turns lighter. "He's got to think of his mate first."

I've been around the block when it comes to romance genres. There isn't too much I shy away from. I recognise the way he uses mate from a science-fiction novel I read a few years ago. It was a totally wild book, but hot as fuck. The author threw around the word mate about every other page. And these guys aren't British or Australian, based on their accents. They don't mean friend.

"Did you drug me?" I croak.

"Just a little to keep you out." He pinches his fingers together to demonstrate, as if that makes me feel any better. "You're a hard nut to crack, ya know that, Walker?"

"What's to crack? I teach science to middle schoolers," I deadpan.

"And you write some really fucked up porn," the other guy snarls like a dog. "You ruined my relationship."

It's on the tip of my tongue to demand how they figured that out. I've always kept Remi Roman out of my personal life. My life as an author has never touched my life as a teacher in the ten years I've been doing both. The few podcasts I've done have been audio only, and my profile pictures are anonymous illustrations I've commissioned. All the world knows about Remi is that she's white and lives on the East Coast.

"I don't know what you're talking about."

"I've got some connections, a few people back in Tolson who were happy to dig a little deeper into your finances," Luca explains. "The dots connected themselves. And poor Nicky here has been devastated since his woman started debasing herself with books like yours. She's an addict, thinks she's better than him."

"Okay, for one, reading adult romances doesn't debase her or whatever fucking shit that is. If I had to guess based on his language and the absolute trash you've been listening to, Nicky here is being a fucking dickhead piece of shit to a lovely person, and she dumped his ass because she knew she could find a better person who respects her."

I realise too late I should have kept my mouth shut. I'm not sure what's got into me, really. This brazen attitude is completely out of character for me, but I can't fucking stand when people hate on romance. It's changed my life in a million different ways, and all of them for the better. The number of readers who have sent me emails and messages about relating to my characters or finally feeling seen in books is unbelievable.

These guys don't get to dictate the narrative.

But they have kidnapped me and are holding me hostage in a dog crate.

Nicky slowly stands up from his chair and starts to strip. I scramble back against the bars. If he touches me, I'm going to rip his dick off. I will fight and claw and kick until my last breath. My fingers curl into fists when he takes his pants down. I look at Luca, his nonchalant pose in the chair unmoved. Have they done this before? Do they take women and assault them for fun? Why would Valentino be friends with someone like this?

There's a glint in his eyes when Nicky crouches down in front of me. The hairs on my arms stand up as something cracks. His body jerks frantically as hair bursts from his skin. Bile rises in my throat when his body grows and creaks like a leather handbag. I'm going to be sick.

His teeth turn sharp, a muzzle where his mouth should be. My lips tremble as terror fills me. Finally, the swishing of a tail is the only sound I hear before my vision starts to fade on the pale grey fucking werewolf in front of me.

I know if I pass out it will be for a few seconds, but maybe I'll hit my head and get some sense knocked into me.

Valentino

What I thought would be a ten-minute wait slowly rolls into thirty and then sixty minutes. There's giving a woman space and then there is walking from one side of the villa to the other in my underwear to see if she's okay. I'm slamming through societal dating goalposts with Cheyenne. I even know that she may be pissed with me come the morning when she realises what I did and do. But more than anything, I know we are meant to be together, and she'll see that too.

It's time to tell her everything.

A few of the boys whistle at me from the kitchen because honestly it's fucking weird seeing me walking around this undressed with no plans to shift. Nonna would kill me if I got hair all over her house, so clearly,

I'm up to something unusual. It's not like I'm sporting a tent in my pants at the moment, but with the way gossip spreads in this family, everyone's going to think we're having some kind of lover's spat.

Outside Andrea and Junelle's suite, my nephew talks quietly on the phone.

"What do you mean he's gone?" he growls, shoulders tensing as his emotions start to run higher. "He's on the fucking schedule for security tonight."

Nobody fucks with Andrea's schedule and gets out of it scot-free. Christ alive, whoever fucked up is going to regret it. He throws his hand out to stop me on my quest to Cheyenne's room, though. What could be so serious about a no-show that he needs my help?

"Keep calling him until he answers. I'll check his suite." He lowers his phone, looking at me like I'm some kind of fucking alien. "What the fuck is going on tonight? No shirt, no shoes, no service."

With how hard my eyes roll, I'm surprised I can still see the smirk that forms on his face.

"Who's the no-show tonight?" I ask instead.

"Nicky. He was scheduled to do twelve hours today, but he just disappeared after dinner. I'm going to go check on him to make sure he's okay and then threaten to put him with Ugo for the rest of the trip for being a pain in my ass."

"Maybe he's having a hard time since Cristina and all that."

Nicky's a good kid most of the time, eager to move up the organisation and prove his worth. We've not had issues with his work ethic before, but he's definitely been off since his long-term girlfriend very publicly and loudly broke up with him a few months ago after she was promoted and he wasn't. From what I recall, Cristina wasn't his mate, so it was for the best anyway that he ripped that band-aid off sooner rather than later.

"I'm really happy for you, Uncle Tino." Andrea's smirk softens, that wistful in-love look coming back over him. Such a fucking lover boy, like his dad used to be.

I'm at a loss for words, awash in memories of my older brother and how much Andrea has grown up to be like him. I pull him into a hug, silently trying to express the well of grief and hope bubbling up inside of me. Today has been a vision of the future, with all of us happy, mated, and together. All I want to do now is wrap myself up in my girl and sleep knowing that our worlds are a little more right than they were before this vacation.

We break apart and start walking in the same direction. While I know where Cheyenne's room is, the rest of the coordinating has been up to Andrea and Nonna. They laid out the villa to be tactically the strongest and most amenable to everyone's needs. That apparently means that Nicky and Cheyenne were placed right next to each other.

While Andrea knocks, I plan to simply open my girl's door. It's locked though, which isn't right. If she's not feeling good after everything that went down today, I want to make sure she's okay. If she's feeling a bit smothered, I want to discuss that. Whatever's going on, I need to know.

I force the door open with my shoulder. Her room is dark, the window open. And it reeks of Luca. Behind me, I hear Andrea force his way into Nicky's room too and then shout in frustration. Something very wrong is happening.

My nostrils flare as my vision starts to turn. Knuckles cracking and teeth growing, I can't force down this rush of anger like I did yesterday. Why the fuck does it smell like him in here? He's supposed to be in Naples.

Where is my mate? I blink twice until the outline of her room becomes clear. Her bed is torn to shreds, but her suitcase is shoved into the corner. The dress she wore tonight hangs on the back of the bathroom door.

Her phone is on the ground.

The change takes over, the fear and rage pushing my body to explode until I'm panting and snarling.

My claws clack against the tiles as I stalk around the room, sniffing and searching for an explanation until I'm standing in front of the open window. A howl rips through my throat, a long call into the night to signal to all who hear it.

Andrea crashes into the room and stares at me. It's not long until more of the family is crowded around the door. My mate has been taken, the rat's nest uncovered.

"Everyone search the grounds," I bark. "Ugo, take Dino and a few others up to the hunting cabin. Kill anyone in your way but bring me Luca."

"What's going on?" Junelle asks, tears forming in her eyes as she sees the carnage. A few of the other human mates look at me with fear.

"Cheyenne's been taken."

We search everywhere. It takes a few hours, but we can't find anything. Marcello tries to locate Luca or Nicky from their phones, but that leads us to the hotel where I had the car parked for the past few days. It's not been a secret where I've been going or who I've been going with.

Up until now, the rat has only been focused on cutting off our imports, weakening our position with the other crime families, and financially trying to ruin our business rather than making it too personal. He hasn't gone after kids or anyone's mate before. It's always been a direct attack on our made men.

But now that I know it's Luca, it makes more sense why certain people were shot or arrested. They were all people he never wanted in the organisation, but who I saw the potential in. Men and women alike he didn't think were strong enough to be wolves. Luca only wanted one type of man in our family, and I refused to listen to his bigotry.

I've been so fucking stupid.

The sun begins to rise. I haven't transformed back, so I've been stalking around the grounds like a feral beast. I can't calm down. Wherever Cheyenne is, I can't feel her. My heart breaks with every passing moment. Two days together and already our connection has become vital to my existence.

"Tino!" Junelle shouts from the back of the villa. "Tino!"

I race through the woods and leap over the stone wall. Junelle and Marcello are standing in the doorway waving me over. I stand as I near them, towering and panting.

"We've found her," Junelle's voice trembles as she presses her thumb on the screen of Cheyenne's phone. It unlocks smoothly and opens onto a map. A little green dot appears in the shape of a pair of headphones. "She must have put them in her pocket."

"She's down at the marina, Tino. How do you want us to proceed?" Marcello asks.

My breathing stutters. We've got her, hopefully. I wrap my arms around them both, unable to stop the racing of my heart.

"Round everyone up," I say when I pull back from the hug. "I want you and Andrea to stay behind with the humans. Junelle, make Nonna show you where the weapons are stored. She won't want to because I know she's still holding onto the grenade launcher I told her to get rid of. I don't want to risk anyone's safety here, but right now we need her to be a bit trigger-happy. Lock everyone in the wine cellar until we're back."

"Do you think Luca is capable of ordering an attack on the villa and taking us on at the same time?" Marcello asks.

"I don't know, but I have every intention of bringing my mate back alive before this wedding."

Outside the marina, my heart freezes in my chest. Fear grips me like it never has before. I'm surrounded by my family, wolves I would trust with my life, but I can't move forward. My breathing turns ragged, the back of the SUV suffocating me. My claws dig into my fur, scratching at something that won't fade away.

I still haven't been able to turn human again. The adrenaline is forcing my body to stay this way, ready to attack, ready to kill. The last shred of my sanity tells me this fear that is caving in my chest is good. It's Cheyenne's fear. It's proof she is very alive and awake.

Focus on that truth, focus on her.

"We've got armed guards wandering the docks," Dino says through the car speaker. "No clue if Luca has turned them, but they haven't noticed me yet."

The fact that these guards can't tell they're boxed in is enough for me. Luca hasn't invested in the strongest men he could find, he's surrounded himself with blind followers. None of these guards will pose a threat too great for him, and therefore too great for us. If what Giuseppe said is true, they've been sold *an idea* of becoming truly powerful, but now they will die for their failures.

"We take them out quietly. Luca most likely knows we are here, but I don't want a police swarm or tourists getting too close. Wait until you see me before you make a move." I signal for Cristina to turn off the car.

Everything quiets.

We move slowly down from the steep incline, past quiet shops and shuttered rental properties. Nobody is awake this early on a Saturday. Even the produce market won't begin setting up in the piazza for another two hours. Nobody notices a giant werewolf or the crew of armed men breaking into the marina.

I rip out the throat of the first man I come upon. He's big and too muscular to be fast. His blood sprays across my front as he tries to breathe his last breath. Around me, Ugo and Dino have partially shifted. They work in tandem, hacking and slashing away. A shot rings out and Cristina drops to her knees, blood dripping down her shoulder.

It doesn't keep her down, though. She transforms, and before I can take two steps towards the fuckwad who shot her, Cristina tears his head from his body. She tosses it onto some poor fisherman's boat and moves on to the next guy.

We have the whole marina cleared out in minutes. Bodies are strewn across the docks. Ugo is pissing on one of them while Dino looks disgusted. Cristina steals the shirt off one of the bodies as she shifts back to her human form.

"Head for the office, they'll be in there," I bark orders. "Leave Luca to me."

It's eerily quiet. A few dogs run out of the building once we pry the doors open, but that's all we hear. This is a small three-story warehouse and resource offices for the marina. There isn't much here, but it's enough to keep us busy searching room after empty room for signs of life.

It's not until we are in the stairwell moving to the final floor that I hear Cheyenne. She's screaming bloody fucking murder. I break ahead of the group on all fours, snarling like a beast to get to my mate.

The top floor is one open room of desks. Luca and Nicky are standing, wolves out and teeth bared as I barrel towards them. Luca and I meet head-on. His claws dig into my fur as I sink my teeth into his shoulder. Nicky jumps on my back and wraps his arm around my throat.

It's like he's learned nothing since he got made. A dog pile isn't going to stop a wolf from protecting their mate. And two rats will never take down the family.

The terror crushing my chest intensifies, burns until all I can think is survive, survive, survive. The others grab Nicky off me, the snarling and barking barely noticeable over the ringing in my ears. Luca kicks my crotch until I choke on his blood and release him.

But as he rolls away from me, a gun goes off. He howls in agony, and then his body begins to convulse when Dino fires his taser into him. Blood pours from his shoulder and his knee as he transforms back into a man. I lick my jowls, panting on my knees as I watch the man who used to be my best friend writhe in pain.

"Hold him down," I growl.

Everyone moves at my order. Luca is barely lucid after the shock, but I don't care. He's going to get exactly what's coming to him for what he's done. I place my claws on his chest and press into his flesh until it rips. Muscles compress and bones splinter as I reach for his heart. I wanted to torture the rat when I caught him, fill his last few hours on earth with suffering for what he has done to our family.

But kidnapping my mate?

I don't care. Luca's words mean nothing to me, and all I want is to see his heart crushed in my fist. He wails, screams, and gnashes until blood gushes between his teeth. He tries to shift, but we're all here crushing one bone after another to prevent the change from happening.

The weak muscle gives a dying pulse as I sink my claws into it.

"Rot in hell," I snarl, with one final yank.

I don't even think about what I'm doing when I tear into his heart. His eyes are empty, his body has stopped twitching. He's dead, but I swallow his heart to make sure it will never taint another being again. He was my best friend, but a rat is a rat.

Luca knew exactly what would happen to him when I found out.

Dino and Ugo drag his corpse out. Cristina grabs Nicky's body next, and I wait for them to leave before

I turn to the rapidly beating heart in the cage tucked into the corner of the room. Her panicky, reedy breaths bombard my senses. The anxiety of the night and the morning weighs down my shoulders.

I'm terrified to look at my mate now. She has seen me for the killer I am. This was never part of the plan. I wanted to show my wolf to her, explain that the first assumptions about Andrea and me were right. We are the mafia, but we are more than that. We would never hurt her, and yet I've put her in so much danger in such a short time.

"Valentino," she whimpers.

Cheyenne

My heart clenches in despair when the giant wolf finally looks at me. His large dark grey head moves, and bright eyes meet mine. I know it's Valentino, my heart knows it's him. The fur covering his body is soaked in blood and viscera, but I reach for him through the bars of the cage.

I need him to reassure me that I'm not going crazy. This is real. He is real. Werewolves are real. Just when I thought everything was falling into place, my world has been blown into a million gory chunks. He can't abandon me now. Not after everything I've seen, right?

"Please," I beg when he stares at me.

Am I wrong? Is this beast someone else? Something else? The horrifying panic of watching men transform and then be murdered fades, the rush of anxiety and terror reshaping into a dull emptiness that I'm scared is swallowing me alive.

"Baby, scoot back," he growls.

His mouth moves like a cartoon, seamlessly perfect, yet it sounds so unnatural coming from his wolf muzzle. His ears draw back as he slowly approaches the cage. A giant fist wraps around the grates of the door.

It's like child's play. One little motion from his wrist, and Valentino has the whole door pried open. He offers me his hand, the roughened dark pads, fur, and claws up close are so different from anything I've seen before, but when I place my hand in his, it's like I've grabbed hold of the last rung of a ladder before I fall into the abyss.

There isn't a breath between our hands meeting and him tugging me into his arms. He clutches me so tightly to his chest I become as soaked as he is. A sob breaks from my lips, and I weep into my werewolf's chest. This is real, I'm alive, and Valentino came for me.

"Tell me you're okay," Valentino demands. "Tell me, Cheyenne?"

He cups both of my cheeks with his oversized paws and pulls me away from him enough to give me a once over.

"This is your blood," I say, scrunching my nose up. "I'm mentally scarred for life, but otherwise in one piece."

"He didn't touch you, did he?" He scowls, the frown lines on his werewolf forehead so impressively normal. "I should have done worse to him."

"Choked, drugged, tied up, tossed in a cage." I list off everything I know happened like it's groceries. "Completely unsexily, by the way. There is no way I'll be able to channel this into a new book."

"Jesus Christ, I'm going to kiss you, and you're absolutely not putting this in a book," Valentino groans.

His lips are on mine before I can tell him how much I need that. They are different from when he's human, but no less intoxicating. My legs wrap around his torso, my arms around his broad shoulders. The emptiness begins to fill, my heart pounding against my chest like it would rather belong to him than to me.

I need more of this, to have my thoughts filled with anything but fear. And when I'm with Valentino, no matter what he's doing, I only feel wanted, needed, like he needs air. He grips my curves so tightly, like he's afraid I'll run away, but there is nowhere else I want to be right now.

"I thought I lost you," he mutters as he breaks the kiss. "I was terrified he'd taken you somewhere I'd never be able to find."

"I'm right here," I promise, running my hands down his fur. As my nails dig in to pull him in for another kiss, he stops me. "Please, Valentino, I need you. Don't make me beg."

"I can't shift right now," he growls like he's trying to force it. "I'm too amped up still, baby. This is going to be me for a while."

"I don't care."

The words come out of my mouth in a rush, and I mean it. Right now, all I want is to be reclaimed.

"You're sure, sweetheart?" His voice takes on a teasing lilt. "You want the monster to fuck your little pussy?"

Heat floods my core in a way I never expected. Yes, yes, I do want him. Human or wolf, Valentino sets me on fire with desire. His claws tease my skin while the fur covering him tickles. My pussy clenches just thinking about the weight of him on me, pressing into me.

"Dirty girl," he whispers, sealing his lips to mine again.

I don't think too hard about the mechanics. I focus on the smell of blood that mixes with air and the pressure of Valentino's dick against my sweatpants.

He's bigger in all ways like this. I slide one hand down his front to wrap my fist around his cock.

The girth has only changed a little, but he's longer now and prelubed. Something swells at the base the longer I feel him. He grunts when I squeeze it, hips jerking up.

"You like my knot?" he asks. "You took it so well the first time, honey, I want to see your face when you sit on it."

"How much of our first time was about me not seeing your dick?"

I gasp when Valentino falls backwards with my knees bracketing his hips. I'm still fully clothed, and as much as I want him to rip my pyjamas off, I also want honesty from him.

"It's why I chose the position I did," he grunts, dragging my hips over his cock. "My knot was so fucking swollen and obvious. I didn't want to scare you."

"But now?"

"Now I want to fuck it so deep into my mate she can't see straight and she's walking out of here safe, well-bred and dripping cum."

My body heats at the idea of leaving this building claimed by this powerful man for all to see. I want the world to know I belong to Valentino Benetti. He has catapulted my life into an otherworldly state of being.

What's real and what matters are different in my head now than they were before I landed.

"Take off my clothes, Valentino," I demand.

He rips my shirt off first. His claws dig into the collar and tear down the middle until I'm hastily shucking it off like a jacket. He pumps his hips until I fall forward, breasts drowning his wolven face. He moans, sucking in a deep breath against my skin.

When he licks one of my nipples, my back arches. Fuck, that feels better than it has any right to. My body hums with pleasure and my pussy clenches. His lips seal around it, and I'm a goner. The mixture of his sharp teeth and textured tongue makes my thoughts slip away. All I can feel is pleasure.

The seam at the crotch of my sweatpants tears like wet paper under Valentino's hands. He snaps the elastic over my hips and shoves each leg down until my knees are padded.

"God, you smell so fucking good," he groans between kissing and licking my other breast. "So fucking hot and wet."

"Fuck me, please. Fill me." I push my ass back, my wet nipples dragging against his fur-covered chest to get me closer to his cock.

He grabs my hips, sharp claws digging into the meat of me as he lines us up. The slick tip of his cock glides through my pussy lips, drenching itself in me.

It nudges my clit, and I squeeze his fur between my fingers with a whimper.

"You know you're mine, Cheyenne."

"Yes." I try to rock my hips enough to get more.

He slots his tip into my hole, and I push down until I reach his swollen knot. The length of him shoots fireworks from my core to my toes until they curl. My eyes flutter closed as my walls spasm.

Valentino controls our pace. He grinds me back and forth, keeping me physically full until the emotional abyss inside of me is full of nothing but him, and us together.

"So fucking gorgeous, baby. Made for me. So perfect. Keep squeezing my dick, just like that, such a good girl for your mate." His voice is rough and tender at the same time. "Gonna move you into my house, gonna fuck so much cum into you, you give me a litter, and we're gonna grow old together. You and me, forever."

My heart jumps into my throat. Yes. Yes, that's what I want. Forever, turning grey and getting wrinkles with my person. Tears of joy and relief threaten to fall, but Valentino cups my cheek, stopping me.

"Feel our connection, Cheyenne. I'm not ever letting go of you. And I'll remind you every day if I have to. I am committed to you, obsessed with you, every little thing about you makes me want you."

The first tear falls as I stare at him, the fullness and the joy inside of me growing exponentially. His heartbeat beneath my hands rings out in my mind, and I feel it. The tendrils of fate that connect us, his devotion and those first beats of love already there.

"I could never have imagined finding someone like you," I whisper.

"Let me show you how real I am."

Valentino holds me tight as he begins to thrust. Our bodies meet in perfect harmony, a collision of fur and skin, a growl and a moan, a werewolf and a human. It's perfect and maddening. My thoughts jumble until I'm moaning nonsense and begging for more.

"Yes, so good, fuck your knot into me. I need your cum, breed me."

His arms wrap around me tightly, holding my exhausted body to his chest as he starts to piston his hips. He fucks me harder and harder, and each time his knot pushes at my pussy.

"Let me in, sweetheart," he moans into my ear, cold nose pressed to my temple. "I know you want to be a dirty girl for me, want to make a mess on my cock and mark my fur with your juices, but you need to breathe."

When did I stop? I gasp, dragging in enough air that when I exhale the coil in my belly loosens. I do it again under Valentino's guidance, his lips and teeth teasing my skin until he's fucking the full swell of his knot into me with every stroke.

The bulge, which presses right behind my clit every time, puts pressure on the sensitive and untouched part of me.

"That's my girl, so fucking proud of you. Taking your mate's cock. Ready for me to breed your little cunt."

"I wanna come," I whine. "Please."

"You will, baby, gotta make it stick, don't we?"

Just as I begin to think he can't get any bigger, Valentino pulls me up from his chest. He slams my body down onto his and begins to rock us together. His knot presses hard on my clit, building a need inside me. I'm gasping for air again, unable to think beyond chasing the feeling. His thumb slides between us, spreading me wider until he's flicking my clit.

My eyes roll back, my body screaming as my lower belly tightens until the world explodes. My pussy gushes, spasms, and sets off a chain reaction. Valentino drives deeper into me as I orgasm. A moan falls from his mouth as his cock shoots ropes of cum into me. His hips shake, and we collapse into each other.

I'm not sure how long we lie there, but his body slowly transforms back into a man. His claws massaging my back turn into fingers. His fur recedes to reveal his soft chest again. The muzzle kissing at my shoulder turns into a soft pair of lips.

It's an easy transition from monster to man. Nothing terrifying this time, even as his bones crack and he shrinks beneath me. It all just feels right.

Except when his cock slides out of me and I'm left holding on to nothing. I groan, the ache of being stretched so far and the feeling of cum sticking to my thigh too much after the time I've had.

"We should get out of here," he murmurs.

"Junelle will be furious if we miss the wedding."

"Gotta shower and nap first." He yawns.

"Take me to your suite then," I say, kissing him.

We hadn't forgotten about the wedding, it's more that we forgot it was happening at the villa. There is a swarm of vans around the drive and flurries of people moving at a fast pace carrying trays and flowers and linens. They're all trying to get this wedding day back on track. Ugo drives us up to the front door, and barks at everyone to scatter before Valentino lets me out of the car.

The shirt he stole from one of the corpses is barely long enough to cover my ass, but it does the job, and I won't have to wear it for long.

Junelle is right there in her bonnet and pristine white wedding robe. She wraps her arms around me without hesitation, the blood on my shirt tacky and mostly dry. We cry big, fat ugly tears. Somewhere behind us men are talking, but they don't matter right now.

"Don't ever scare me like that again," she sniffles.

"I won't," I promise. "Not in a million years do I wanna do that again."

"So you know now," she says after another round of crying. "Explains a lot, doesn't it?"

I nod because of course it doesn't, but I'm too relieved to be back on solid ground to care about all the questions I still have. Junelle let go of our embrace only to pull me into another hug. Neither of us can stop crying, but soon my head starts to pound and my ears are ringing.

"We need to get inside," Valentino whispers to us. "And you have a wedding to get dressed for."

He and Andrea usher us back into the house, splitting us in the foyer as Junelle goes to get cleaned up and to continue all her wedding prep. Valentino picks me up bridal style at the base of the stairs and carries me all the way to the shower in his suite.

Even as he turns the water on, he doesn't put me down.

"You're going to have to let me go so we can clean up," I say.

He grumbles but does it. Valentino removes my clothes carefully before pulling the shower head down. Blood melts from our skin as the warm water cascades around us. He does all the work: rinsing, washing, shampooing, conditioning, washing again to make sure there isn't a speck of our last twelve hours on us. His touch is gentle as he dries us off, he even applies lotion to my skin. I feel like a whole new person by the time I'm sitting with my back against the headboard.

"Your neck's bruising pretty badly," he mutters. "Let me get you some ice."

"Ibuprofen too, please." I yawn.

Valentino doesn't leave the room. Instead, he leans his head out the door and shouts. Within moments he has what he asked for.

"Were you raised in a barn?" I take the water and pills offered to me. It's harder to swallow than I realised it would be. There's a very disturbing part of me that wants to take notes on these feelings. Write everything down even though I will remember what this feeling is like for the rest of my life.

"No," he huffs, scowl firmly set on his face. This might be the grumpiest I have seen him all vacation, which feels insane given that he beat the shit out of a guy. This should be the time when he smiles, right? I survived and he successfully rescued me. Happily ever after acquired.

Valentino gently places a towel filled with ice at the base of my neck. I suck in a sharp breath as a chill runs down my spine. He keeps staring at me, eyes unwavering as I slowly adjust to the cold. He holds my hands in one of his while he watches me. For a long while, I stare back at him, waiting to see what he'll do or say. When it feels like an eternity has passed and icy droplets dribble down to my navel, I break the tension.

"So, are you born that way?" I ask.

"No," he grunts.

"Does it hurt?"

"Only the first time. You need to rest your voice, Cheyenne, and try to sleep." His tone suggests I listen, but I take it as what it is, a suggestion.

"What came first? The mob or the wolfie?"

"The wolf, but we've been in this business for a very, very long time."

"Stability is good." I crack a smile. "So, is it like the meme? Do you have two wolves inside of you?"

"Fuck's sake, sweetheart." He shakes his head, but I can tell he's trying not to smile. "It's still me when I'm in my wolf. I'm just bigger and hairier and more myself, I guess."

"Is everyone but me and Junelle a wolf?" I settle down at his insistence. Definitely making a mental note about bondage though.

"No, all the mates here are still human. It's a weird magic biology thing. When we bite our mates, they become tied to us instead of turning."

"What's a mate?" I think I know the answer to this, but I want him to tell me, anyway. No more secrets.

"It's a fated, celestial bond between a supernatural creature and a human. Werecreatures know our mates by scent. The night you arrived at the villa, I was in the woods, and I could smell you. I knew you were mine right then and there."

"There are more than just werewolves?" My eyes become heavy with exhaustion, but my curiosity is begging me to stay awake. I want to know everything. A new layer of the world has revealed itself to me. The analytical side of my brain wants to discover it all.

"Close your eyes, and I'll start listing them off," Valentino whispers, a smile finally cracking on the corner of his lips. Once my eyes are closed, he pulls the covers up over me and starts to list them softly. "Wolves, bears, bison, gators, boars..."

I wake with a start, my body locking up as a warm arm pulls me in tighter. Valentino hums behind me until my brain has caught up with the fact I'm not in a cage anymore. The abyss I felt hours ago threatens to swallow me whole again. My body aches with an emptiness, a need to feel claimed and reclaimed.

"I'm right here, sweetheart," Valentino whispers.

There are blankets between us though, soft and warm, but the opposite of what I need. I want his skin on mine. I want his rough hands to grip the parts of me I haven't learned to love yet while he tells me I'm his. I want to have all of him crush me into his bed until he is the only thing I can see.

"Should I be more scared?" I ask, trying to push my heated thoughts to the side.

"What do you mean?" Valentino cups my cheek as I roll to face him. He's still naked, but from the dark circles under his eyes, he hasn't taken a nap like I have.

He peels the covers back and pulls me into his lap. He cradles me into his chest, but this isn't the comfort I need right now. And that's what scares me. I feel almost normal. The only thing about me that doesn't feel the same as yesterday afternoon is that my throat hurts.

"I watched a pack of werewolves kill two other werewolves, and you ate a man's heart!" I say, flabbergasted. "Shouldn't I be a little grossed out or worried?"

"Wolves don't really get blood-borne illnesses, so I mean that's not a concern. But as for being scared, I will do whatever it takes to make you feel safe, Cheyenne."

"That is the most realistic experience I could ask for as a writer. But this is what I mean. I'm not *that* traumatised."

"Do you want to be?"

"No," I whine.

"Take this as a sign from the universe." He smiles as he kisses my forehead. "You're exactly as prepared as you need to be, and right now all we need to do is get dressed and enjoy a wedding."

"Will you dance with me?"

"Until the end of time," he promises.

The microphone is heavy in my hand. Sweat beads across my forehead, drips down my back as I stare at my family and the close friends of the Benettis. We are crammed into the backyard, the hard decking over the pool turned into a dance hall. It's gorgeous. You'd never think I had this place torn apart twelve hours ago.

It's my time to give a speech.

"Thank you, everyone, for joining us at our ancestral home as we add another beautiful person to our family. Can we get another round of applause for Junelle?" I pause, letting the attention move back to the bride so I can take a calming breath. My gaze flicks just to my right where Cheyenne sits in her stunning plum dress. Elation plays at my heartstrings when she smiles at me. "I won't give a long speech, I know the staff have prepared a good meal for us. Andrea, you've grown into a man right before my eyes, but you're still just the little boy who used to make me pinky promise on everything we made. It didn't matter if it was to have ice cream after dinner or to come home after work, you wouldn't leave my side without that promise."

I walk around the head table to my nephew, my heir, to the man I raised with all the love I could as a man stricken with grief and rage. He's already leaning forward when I get to him. Tears slip down his cheek as I hook my pinky around his.

"I promise that all the Benetti here and in our hearts are so proud of the man you've become. Promise me you'll spend the rest of your life showing Junelle what a good man you are?"

"I promise," he murmurs, hand shaking, before he stands and hugs me over the table. "Thank you, Uncle Tino."

"Love you, kid." My voice is harsh with how much I'm holding back tears.

I hug Junelle next, and the waterworks just come out of me. The tears start falling, and I don't give two shits. I've got to be the luckiest fucking man in the world. My family is the most beautiful creation. Perfect even when we're messy.

I sniffle hard once I'm standing back enough to see everyone again. "Now, let's eat!"

Waitstaff appear in the blink of an eye, setting plates in front of everyone at the head table. I pull Cheyenne's seat closer to mine when I sit down. She hands me a tissue as she dabs her eyes. The makeup team really did a masterclass amount of work to cover up the bruising on her neck. I kiss her forehead. She won't ever need to cover up again.

"That was a lovely speech," she says, her voice still a little too broken for my liking.

I pass her a glass of ice water. She's not exactly pleased I said we weren't drinking tonight, but I promised to make it up to her later.

"You should have seen him in Jamaica," Ugo laughs, taking a slurp from his wineglass. "Never thought he'd stop crying."

Cristina slaps his shoulder. "Don't be a dick, or we'll make your wedding worse."

"Psh, who says I want all this?" He rolls his eyes. Ugo has just turned thirty, he's got his whole life ahead of him, yet he's got it in his head he doesn't have a mate. A defence mechanism if I've ever seen one. We've all got our crazy vices. His future mate won't see those as red flags, though.

Like Cheyenne has, she's seen me at my most feral yet. She still wants me, craves to be near me, even after everything she saw this morning.

"You don't have to have this exactly," Cheyenne says. "I don't want this exactly. It's a whole societal construct to control women. As if a piece of paper will speak louder than my or my partner's actions?"

"Oh, no, I want the whole thing." Cristina puts her elbows on the table as a wistful look appears on her features. "Swept off my feet, the dress, the vows. If my mate doesn't sob like a baby while my dad walks me down the aisle, I don't want 'em."

Conversation carries on. I ask about her father, who retired from the life a while back and is living in the middle of the woods. Like always, this starts Cristina off on a tirade of complaints. It allows my thoughts to drift to what Cheyenne said. She wants a partner whose actions will speak louder than words. While I feel like I have proven that about myself, if I had to guess, it's about sustained actions.

I can do that.

Step one is dancing with my mate as promised.

As the DJ begins to play, I hold out my hand for Cheyenne. Her hand is warm, firmly grasping mine as I guide us through the small crowd to the dance floor. Junelle winks at her as we pass by. I imagine she's blushing under all that makeup if what I'm feeling is an indicator.

There is nothing particularly special about this dance. The music is slow, so we mostly sway in lazy steps around the edge of the dance floor. Cheyenne holds me tight, her fingers curling around the hair at the base of my neck as my hand flexes around the voluptuous curve of her waist.

She tenses for a moment, but then she looks at me. Her soft eyes glisten under the lights. I see our whole future mapped out in them. The love that's already growing between us flourishing back home. The push and pull of my lifestyle feeding into her writing. I want to be her muse, the man she turns to when she needs inspiration. Whatever she needs from me for her to succeed, I'll give it to her.

"You're thinking very hard," she whispers as the song fades into another.

"Move in with me," I say. "You can do whatever you want but let me come home to you every day."

"You really wanna see all my dirty secrets, don't you?"

I crack a smile as heat flares in my chest. "You're my dirty girl, aren't you?"

Cheyenne laughs, loud and full of life. There isn't a care in the world behind that noise. She is utterly, completely content.

"Are we going to share an office?" she asks. "I need somewhere to display all my spicy art."

"You can hang up any art you want, baby," I promise, leaning down to her ear so only she can make out what I'm saying. "I'm sure I'll be able to help with your creative process."

I kiss across her jaw, carefully on her neck. Her breath hitches, her fingers tightening on my neck as we slow to a stop. My dick is half hard, pressing against my trousers as we stare at each other.

"What if I'm feeling inspired right now?"

Her breath ghosts across my cheek and sends a chill right down my spine.

"Tell me what you're thinking."

"I'm thinking I'd like a do-over of our first time," she says softly. "I want to experience those feelings again with the knowledge I now have, how you envisioned it happening."

The wolf side of me is practically panting at the opportunity.

"My dirty girl wants me to claim her good, doesn't she?"

Cheyenne doesn't say anything, but her arousal pounds through our bond. The rush she feels when I call her mine makes my head spin.

"I'll give you a head start. Go up to my suite while I say good night," I say. She turns to leave, but I tug her back to me just as fast. "Not before I get a taste of your pretty mouth."

Her lips part, and I kiss her long and slow. My hand slides over her bare shoulder, grazing that invisible little scar she already carries. I'm going to make it last tonight, one she'll see every day, to remind her that she belongs to me.

Just like that first night, I tap her ass as she leaves. I quickly say good night to Andrea and Junelle. We're still on for breakfast in the morning, but I'm leaving the party earlier than I originally planned.

Marcello catches my eye as I've nearly escaped, two small glasses of limoncello in his hands. He comes up quickly, a nervous look in his eyes. I swear I can't take anymore shit today. Our little vacation turned into a whirlwind of chaos. Why can't we enjoy the peace for just a moment?

"Hey boss, I need to ask you something." He doesn't offer me the other drink, and I'm wondering if he needed the second one for courage.

"If it's work, it can wait," I tell him, moving to step around him.

"It's not bad." He clears his throat as he steps in front of me. Marcello squares his shoulders, and swallows. "I want to transfer to Tolson."

I pause.

"With Luca out of the picture now, you'll need someone to take over his role. I'm not asking to be your second. I'm sure that's Andrea and I'd never want to step on anyone's toes, but I want to do more with the family. If you had someone else in mind, maybe they could take my spot here, ya know? Really teach them what it means to be a part of the Italian mob. Nonna could really use some young wolves around the villa to keep her busy."

I smirk. She'd eat most of our made men alive if she got the chance. She doesn't do much with the business side of the family these days. I imagine if I asked her to train up some of our younger members, she'd gleefully accept putting them in their place.

"I'll have the consigliere get your papers sorted when I'm back."

"Really?" he asks. Marcello really has me questioning if I'm that much of an asshole. I need another tested capo I can trust stateside, why not him? There are a few people I'd be happy to promote, but I like the idea of having them prove themselves first.

"Yes." I clap him on the shoulder, trying to end the conversation.

"Here, we toast." He finally offers me the second drink.

"Have a drink for my health," I chuckle. "I've got a mate who needs claiming."

I head into the house. The air conditioning hits my heated skin, but it doesn't do anything to cool the arousal burning inside of me. I take the stairs to the second floor two at a time in a rush to get to Cheyenne.

The door is unlocked.

And she's just stepping out of the bathroom, makeup wipe still in hand as she removes all the foundation off her neck. Her shoes are off, and she looks so much more relaxed. She's still in her dress, though. The material clings to her skin, the neckline just hinting at the swell of her breasts.

"I didn't want to get makeup everywhere," she smiles. "And it doesn't really hurt as much as it did earlier."

"Benefits of being mated," I say, slowly approaching her. "You should heal up much quicker, but we still need to be gentle."

"Yeah," she sighs. "I don't think I'm going to want to try choking anytime soon."

I take the wipe from her hand and smooth it across her skin. Nearly all her freckles are visible again, as are the tan lines from days in the sun. The flush on her cheeks is vibrant and beautiful.

"Let's talk about the vision." I toss the wipe and turn her around. "If I'm going to be your muse, I want to make sure we get it all out."

As I slide the zipper down her back, I lean into her. My body looms over hers as I bare my mate. I see her pulse jump at the base of her neck. She's so beautiful, so unbelievably perfect for me in ways she might not even realise yet. But I have time to show her, to prove to her over and over again how meant for each other we are.

"I want you on all fours for me, sweetheart."

She nods, turning her head just slightly to look into my eyes.

"I'm going to fuck your slutty, soaked hole until you can't think of anything but me. Until the only word that can come out of your pretty lips is my name. When I mount you, knot you, I'm going to claim you as mine forever all over again. There's no going back from it."

Her dress falls to the floor, and I unclasp her bra. She whimpers, and I'm worried it's from the red marks it left behind. How fucking tight was that thing? But she's already rushing to peel off her shapewear. They material rolls down to reveal her supple, dimpled thighs. The smell of her arousal coats the suite.

Cheyenne crawls into the bed before I've even undone my tie.

"Are you going to be a good girl and take my cum?"

"Yes, Valentino." Her voice is so sure, so warm. "I want all of you, mafia boss, werewolf, and everything else in between."

"Do you want your vibe?" I strip quickly, staring at her ass the whole time. "You might be the one to hold it."

She bites her lip. "Maybe, if that's okay?"

I pull her suitcase over, and she digs through it until she gets the toy. She sets it between her legs, just within reach.

My body thrums with electricity, with desire to breed my mate. I stand on the side of the bed once I'm naked, cock hard and knot visible. I carefully move Cheyenne's hair out of her eyes and guide her to look at me.

"Whatever you need from me, baby, I'll give it to you," I promise.

"I'm going to die from the anticipation if you don't fuck me soon," she says, cheeks burning bright.

"Can't have that, can we, not when I'm supposed to be inspiring the next great American novel."

Cheyenne bursts with laughter again, reaching for me with one hand. She kisses my knuckles before drawing them towards her face.

"Forever here we come," she says.

I smooth my thumb over her cheek for a moment, then step behind her. God, I don't think I will ever get tired of this view. Her back arches as I take each of her ass cheeks in hand and spread her open. Her tight little asshole flutters and her cunt drips with her arousal. If I weren't so keen on putting my cum in her pussy, maybe I'd consider anal one day, but I'm not sure it will ever be as good as her wet heat.

I smear two fingers in her juices, teasing her clit for just a few strokes before I plunge them into her. Cheyenne's pussy squeezes me tight as she moans. I pump my fingers into her, relishing the sounds she makes as her body loosens up for me.

"Oh fuck," she whimpers when my fingers crook downward towards her G-spot.

"Does my little slut like my fingers?" I grip her ass tighter.

Fluid drips down my hand as I continue to fuck her with my fingers. My teeth ache and drool forms in the back of my mouth at the sight of it. I want to drink her up. To waste something as delicious as my mate's arousal is basically a crime.

I pull my fingers out just when I think she's about to climax, when her toes curl and her breathing stops. I want her loose, desperate for my knot when I finally give it to her. Just like on that first night, she needs to beg for my cum.

So I drop to my knees and lick up all her juices as if I were worshipping at the altar, slowly ravishing her pussy lips and sucking on her clit as she tries to hump my face. She's desperate for release, I know, but I can't bring myself to stop tasting her.

"Valentino," she whines.

A growl rumbles in the back of my throat. She's my prey for the moment, the predator in me wants to pounce, but she needs to say the words. "Use your words for me, dirty girl."

"Fuck me."

"I thought I was just doing that?" I lick her from clit to asshole, watching the shiver race up her spine.

"I want you to fuck your knot into me," she moans. "I want you to claim me and breed me and fuck me full of little wolves."

My dick leaks at her words. Fuck I didn't realise how close I was just from eating her pussy. I stand again and spread her open. There isn't any ceremony or teasing. I line up the tip of my dick with her dripping cunt and thrust. Her wet heat envelops me, squeezes me so tight I think I might be about to see God myself.

"Jesus Christ," she gasps, cunt gripping my shaft like it's the only thing keeping her alive.

"'S not my name, baby, but it's going to mean the same thing once we're done."

Cheyenne

Can you choke on dick even when it's in your pussy?

That's what it feels like is happening. Valentino pulls his cock out just to thrust into me again, and I see stars. Every part of my body hums as he works into a rhythm. I'm shaking with need and desire as he fucks me.

My elbows bend as I struggle to keep myself up. Valentino adjusts to accommodate me though, putting one of his feet on the bed as he starts pulling my hips back to meet his thrusts. His knot presses hard against my pussy. My heart hammers against my chest.

I'm so close to coming. I could grab my wand, using my vibrator to make us both finish, but something inside of me is telling me this isn't enough. I want more of Valentino.

"Please," I beg, pushing myself back hard against his knot.

"Please what, sweetheart?"

He leans over me, forcing my shoulders down, and I feel the difference in him. Unlike the first night, his growth is more prominent. The hair on his body is more like fur, and his hand still on my hip becomes tipped with claws rather than nails.

I moan, low and pitiful, when I turn my head and see his muzzle.

"Put your baby in me," I whimper. "Breed me."

Words that I've never written or even thought of as sexy now come spilling out of me. Valentino growls against the back of my neck as he does exactly what he said he would. He mounts me, fucking me so hard I'm worried the bed frame is going to shatter.

It doesn't stop him, though.

"That what my dirty girl needs?" he grunts. "Pussy full of her mate?"

"Yes!"

"That's fucking right." His hips snap harder and harder, pounding me until I can't see straight. "Grab your vibe, baby, make this little pussy cream."

I fumble for it, finger jamming all the buttons until it roars to life. The moment it touches my hot, wet skin, my world goes blank. My limbs sizzle with euphoria as my orgasm crashes through me. There's a shout, whether it's mine or Valentino's or both of us, I don't know. I just know that as my clit spasms, my stretched cunt fills with cum.

Sharp teeth sink into my shoulder, and my body jerks. The smell of blood hits my nose, but there's only a pinch of pain. The wand on my clit is prolonging my climax to the point I'm worried I'll never walk straight again.

Valentino's knot pulses, his shaft flexes, and spurts of cum threaten to inflate me like a balloon as if I'm not already floating on cloud nine. He groans against my shoulder, keeping me pinned down as my body verges on overstimulation.

He removes his teeth, and I drop my vibrator. I can't feel my fingers or my toes. My body shakes as Valentino licks up the blood around my shoulder. He shifts onto one elbow and slides his other hand beneath me. He caresses my tummy, the bloated feeling all the more obvious now.

And I let him. I don't feel any worry as he loves on my body. Every stroke and brush of his claws carries another promise of the future.

"Such a beautiful mate," he whispers. "My pretty little slut."

"You'd be a slut for this dick too," I giggle. "It's magic."

He barks with laughter. As I struggle to keep my eyes open, Valentino slides us up his bed still connected. He arranges the pillows and duvet until we are cocooned in them. My fingers twirl around the fur of his arm while he nuzzles against my throat.

"Thank you," I murmur.

"For what?" he asks.

"Being exactly as you are."

The attendant at Naples Airport looks at me, then his gaze flicks back to Valentino. I told him it was fine, we could just meet at the airport back in Tolson. He refuses to let me fly economy when he literally hired a private jet for this trip. If the rest of the Benettis are flying home this way, so am I.

"And you're sure you want to cancel this ticket?" he asks again.

"Yes, please." I nod, aware that I'm only carrying my small backpack at the moment and that I'm somewhat slathered in foundation to hide the yellowing bruises around my neck. I look suspicious, and anyone with eyes would think that. But honestly, I'm dying to get out of economy seating. Junelle said the jet is a luxury she never wants to give up.

I may also want to see if the mile high club is worth it.

"She's already been confirmed as a passenger on our flight manifest," Valentino growls, his voice hard. "It will be in your system."

The man blanches slightly and rapidly types away. I glance over my shoulder and see the scowl on Valentino's face. I want to tease him, but I keep my lips zipped tight while the agent confirms everything is now in order. Airports are not the place to cause problems, period.

The gate agent hands me a new boarding pass that doesn't have any information on it. Just my name and time of departure.

"Thank you," I say as he hands back my passport with a weird stamp in it. "Have a nice day."

Valentino silently guides me past the mile-long crowds to a nearly empty desk. Except for the other Benettis.

"Head count," Andrea orders. He raises his hand and starts to count. Junelle throws her arm over my shoulder, and I wrap mine around her waist.

"I'm not ready for the real world yet," I grumble.

"Same, but it's really not that bad when you remember who your boyfriend is."

"Eighteen, we're all here, let's head out."

All of us flying back tonight are led through more emptiness in an airport that was just heaving with people. We don't go through security, and a customs officer speaks to us on this side of the border. It's almost blissfully easy being whisked through the entire airport without an ounce of anxiety.

A bus takes us across the tarmac, and we climb the steps onto the plane. Vacation over. It's back to the real world of deadlines, papers, and screaming kids who test my patience. As we take off, Valentino squeezes my hand tight.

"This is the rest of our forever."

I look at his shimmering brown eyes and see the same contentment that I feel. I can't wait to live my life with this mafia boss, werewolf and all.

Cheyenne

Epilogue

Six Months Later

"Cheyenne," Valentino shouts from downstairs.

I can't listen. I'm so close to being done with this new manuscript. I'm so close. The words are flowing right out of me, and if I stop now, I might not ever be able to pull them back. We can't have that. My readers are dying for this book.

I'm dying for this book, more importantly.

Something about it has just come so naturally.

Maybe it's all that inspiration I've been getting. Not just the mind-blowing sex, but now when I'm not sure if a murder plot or fight scene makes sense, I've got a team of guys happy to tell me how to make it more real. Whether it's bones breaking or blood gushing, Ugo and Dino are always eager to share what they know with me.

"Honey, Junelle is here," Valentino says, leaning against the door to our shared office.

In a short time, I've littered this space with so much character art. If anything, being given free rein has made me commission even more art. It's so heartwarming and grounding seeing two of my imaginary idiots fucking when I'm having a bad day. I keep all the naughty art on my side of the room so Valentino can still have his calls and work without scandalising anyone, but big and proud just behind his chair is a movie poster size print out of *His Ballerina's Secret*.

I cried when I first saw it. It never occurred to me before that I could treat my covers that way, with such reverence. But seeing that on a random evening after a particularly stressful day in the classroom had me ugly crying in an instant. I suddenly felt like a professional, and not just a hobbyist.

"Baby," Valentino whispers in my ear. He pulls my wheelie chair away from the desk and turns me to face him. "Your best friend is downstairs to see you. You're having dinner, remember?"

"Just—"

"No. You've spent all day in here. It's time to stretch and rest your eyes and eat something that isn't covered in chocolate."

"But those were fruit," I argue, standing with a groan.

"Chocolate-covered raisins are not fruit."

"Who's got the science degree here?" I put my hands on my hips.

He snorts and then kisses my forehead before he leads me out of the room. As if passing a magical barrier, when I leave the office, I suddenly race to get down the stairs in Valentino's house. Well, our house now. My name is also on the deed.

Homeownership might be as big of a surprise as the werewolf thing, honestly. Who would have thought?

"And here we see a gremlin, emerging from her cave to search for nourishment and companionship." Andrea announces my arrival like I'm some chipmunk in a nature documentary. He and Junelle burst into laughter when I stick my tongue out at both of them. Junelle quickly pulls me into a hug.

They've been on their second honeymoon, and despite being back for a couple months, we've all been too swamped with work to get together. It's amazing that even though we live in the same city, it's so easy to go ages without seeing our family. Valentino's made a whole lasagne for the occasion, the delicious smell wafting through the hallways as we walk to the kitchen.

"Wine?" I ask.

"None for me," Junelle says.

"Yeah, I've got to get up early tomorrow." Andrea pulls out a barstool from the counter. "I don't want to pick up Enzio with wine sweats. He's gonna be fucking feral tomorrow as it is."

"How long has he been away?" I ask, pouring glasses for me and Valentino.

He takes his glass and lightly taps it against mine before he takes a drink. Plates are warming in the oven, and we're just waiting for the lasagne to rest before we cut into it. He didn't even bother making anything else. Apparently, it's just that good.

"Twelve months now?" Andrea guesses.

"It's a damn miracle we're still running. Just proof we need to get someone to help him." Valentino sighs. Whoever Ezio is, he's got my mate in knots about this upcoming team expansion. I don't know why he wouldn't want more help. It's wildly insecure that not a single other person in the Benetti Crime Family knows the ciphers and codes to run the finances. "They don't have to like each other, they just need to work together."

"Have you decided if you're going to do another year at school?" Junelle asks, changing the subject.

This launches me into a huge, long discussion about the pros and cons of leaving my full-time job. Valentino has listened to me having this same conversation with myself over and over again since the fall semester started. It's only got more stressful as we near midterms.

I don't pay for anything now. In true book boyfriend fashion, as the movers carried my boxes into his house, Valentino handed me a debit card and a credit card. Those are for my everyday purchases. He also set up an account in my name only, that has money paid into it monthly for me to use for emergencies or to keep me living comfortably if anything were to happen.

As if my book money hasn't been the thing funding my retirement for years, anyway.

But there is something about taking this jump that I am scared to do. I spent years at college getting my degree, years in the classroom working with nightmare preteens. It feels like I'm throwing a part of myself away by leaving teaching. It's stressful, more so every day, but it's been my security blanket for years.

"Oh, thinking of next summer," Junelle says well after our conversation had moved on to book plans and the store-bought brownies I bought yesterday in a fit of sugar deprivation. "I can't be your assistant next July."

"What?" I garble, brownie stuck to the roof of my mouth. I only just paid our deposit for us to go. It wasn't expensive, but that con is supposed to be our thing. A first for both of us. I take a drink of my wine to clear my mouth.

"Well, I don't think a newborn is really going to be helpful," she explains.

I spew my drink across the table. Thankfully, it doesn't spray anyone, but oh my god.

Oh my god!

Valentino stands so fast his chair falls over as he rushes to get to Andrea. He hugs him tight, and I don't know what they are saying, but I hear the sniffles. Once I've cleaned myself up enough, I launch myself at Junelle too. Every bit of love I have for her, I pour into this hug.

"Congratulations, I'm so excited for you," I murmur. "You'll be such a great mom."

"Well, when they'll have an auntie like you," she says.

My breath catches and tears drip down my cheek. I pull back and look at Junelle, her eyes misting with tears. She cracks a smile, then I'm giggling, and soon it's a screaming fest of excitement because my best friend is having a baby. I'm going to be an auntie.

Valentino wraps both of us in another hug, Andrea closing up our little circle. We stand like that for a long while, our familial embrace making me cry all the more. The love I feel for everyone here is so overpowering. Nothing could tear us apart.

"How far along are you?" I ask Junelle.

"Ten weeks, but I couldn't wait another two. I needed to tell you. It's been eating me alive keeping this a secret."

As we wind down for the night, it's hard to say goodbye. I know we will see them again soon, we've got a whole homecoming dinner planned for Ezio in a week's time, but my clinginess and anxiety are begging me to latch on to my best friend. She will text me when she gets home. We'll video call when she's on her lunch break tomorrow.

Our friendship will always be here, growing and changing until we are the coolest old ladies at the villa. I know this, but I still hug her extra tight.

"Text me when you get home safe."

"And text me when you finish that last spicy scene," she says, squeezing me tight before she and Andrea walk out the door.

Valentino and I clean up the kitchen, pouring ourselves another glass of wine to kill the bottle. We're quiet as we come down from the news, but I feel his excitement and worry through our bond. I've got a lot better at picking apart our emotions, but tonight there is nothing to sort through. We feel the same thing.

I take his hand and guide him into our bathroom.

"We deserve a bath," I say.

"You read my mind."

Slowly, we peel off layers of clothes, constantly stopping to touch. Neither of us is very good at separation. We crave physical touch. I need his hands on me, grounding me, reminding me that he's just as obsessed with me as I am with him.

Valentino climbs into the steaming tube first, holding his hand out for me to sit in front of him. The heat makes my skin tingle and flush. I pass him his glass of red and lean back. His skin is hot, hairs tickling me as his legs squeeze around my body.

We sigh in unison.

I raise my glass slightly. "To family."

"To romance books." Valentino grins, and I can't help but agree.

To making your book boyfriend a reality.

THANK YOU FOR READING!

T hank you for reading *Claimed by the Werewolf Boss*. This story is a wild romp inspired by my own boring holiday in Italy that involved a wedding. Sadly, no werewolves for me though. If you're interested in more monstrous characters and plus size love interests, check out my other books through my website: authorashraven.com/links

If you liked this book, please remember to leave a review on your preferred sites to help other readers find my work.

LOVE TO THE RAVEN'S NEST

A big thank you to all my Patreon supporters, with special shout out to:

Jenna, Kelly, Morally_Gray_Nola, tentacularly, Jacquelyn C, Raelyn, Justice, Debi EB, Kassandra B, Cassandra LR, Amanda, chibigoatess, Amber R, Sue, Lauren B, Emmy L, Tysharina, Heather S, Dajana S, Shell, Jemmique M, ilana c, Aden, lovetostitch, Heather K, Emily S, Alexandria C, bree, AIM, Kitty, Sarah U, Christine, TiffTerr, Melanie R, Kbucky, Faye, Biscuitquick

ALSO BY ASH RAVEN

Check out the Sins of The Flesh series.

The Librarian of Souls
The Pirate Queen of Ruin
The Widow of Fortune
The Kingpin of Magic

Check out the First Date Abductions series.

Jumping the Shark: Matched with the Space Shark

Check out the Hallow's Cove series.

Wolves and Whipped Cream

About the Author

Ash Raven is an indie author who specialises in spicy monster and alien romances that focus on plus-size and LGBTQ+ leads who get the love of a lifetime. They strive to write stories that are inclusive and real, with a touch of magic and a boat load of spice. When they are not writing, they are cuddling with their two orange cats and drinking oat mochas through a straw. They have been living their own insta-love romance in London, UK since 2015.

Want to know more? You can find Ash on most social media as @authorashraven or subscribe to their newsletter for exclusive updates, art prints, and cat pictures.